THE ART
OF DYING

THE ART OF DYING

Diana Killian

To order additional copies of this book, contact:
Xlibris Corporation
1-888-7-XLIBRIS
www.Xlibris.com
Orders@Xlibris.com

CONTENTS

CHAPTER ONE 9
CHAPTER TWO 23
CHAPTER THREE 33
CHAPTER FOUR 43
CHAPTER FIVE 58
CHAPTER SIX 73
CHAPTER SEVEN 90
CHAPTER EIGHT 105
CHAPTER NINE 125
CHAPTER TEN 139
CHAPTER ELEVEN 151
CHAPTER TWELVE 164
CHAPTER THIRTEEN 178
CHAPTER FOURTEEN 192

To Larry and Karla Stark—with much love.

CHAPTER ONE

Tall, dark and silent he stood amidst the sun hats and boogie boards queued for the bus to Steeple Hill.

Hilary's fingers itched for the charcoal and sketchpad in her knapsack. She took quick mental notes, planning to draw from memory later. Beautiful bones: cheek bones, jaw line, and that nose . . . perfect. Daniel perhaps? Or no, a young Solomon. That dark forelock falling across his pale forehead hinted at a passionate nature beneath the reserved exterior.

The body wasn't bad either. Long, lean and broad-shouldered. Maybe a little overdressed for the beach in a tailored shirt and leather boots. He was the only person not wearing sunglasses, and as Hilary studied him he put a hand up to his eyes as though the bright light hurt.

That slight gesture altered Hilary's perspective. She saw before her a man, not a subject. Not a model. A man in pain.

She glanced away, uncomfortable for a moment; her eyes followed the dazzle of the sunlight on the ocean.

The next moment the bus rumbled up in a cloud of dust, spewing fumes like an asthmatic dragon waiting as the crowd shuffled on board. Hilary shouldered her knapsack, and grabbed her sketch pad. She followed the man up the bus steps.

Inside, the bus was hot as an oven and crowded. The noise seemed to bounce off the metal ceiling. The air was thick with the scent of perspiration and suntan oil. Hilary was braced for it; the man ahead of her hit it like a wall. She saw him reach for the steel pole, knuckles whitening. She saw too that the knuckles of his hand were scraped and puffy.

"Seventy five cents," said the bus driver without looking up.

The man stood still, slowly patting the pockets of his Levi's. Finally he had his wallet out; he proffered a crisp bill.

"Exact change, buddy," the bus driver said, bored.

One hand still clenched around the bus pole, the man leaned into the bus driver's face. He said something low-voiced.

The driver was a big man but he shrank back in his seat, eyes pinned to the other's face. The man straightened and with deliberation stuffed the bill into the token box.

"Suit yourself, buddy!" said the bus driver.

The man turned away.

The incident took less than a minute. No one around Hilary seemed to notice. Hilary paid her fare and followed the man down the crowded aisle, picking her way through beach chairs, boom boxes and bare legs. Ahead of her the man half-fell over an ice chest and dropped into one of the last empty seats.

Hilary slid her sketchbook and knapsack into a seat the row behind his. Her view was partially obscured by a woman wearing a floppy sun hat. Through the plastic oranges and cherries Hilary watched as the man's head fell back against the metal frame of the seat. For a few moments he stayed very still, barely breathing, lines carved around his mouth and nose, eyes closed but lashes flickering.

The doors hissed shut and Hilary made herself look away. The bus shuddered like an animal shaking itself, and lumbered off the shoulder of the road. Hilary told herself that he did not look like a man to welcome interference, however well-meant. She told herself it was none of her business.

The old bus rattled and bounced its way down the winding coast road back to town. To the right the ocean stretched in endless fields of glittering blue fading off into the white haze of the afternoon sun. It was spring, and the California hills blazed with gold. Hilary lost herself in the shimmering effect of poppies and mustard flowers rippling in the breeze off the sea. Burnt umber, cadmium, Naples yellow: the colors of warmth, birth, abundance and resurrection. Of course it was easy to get carried away with the symbolism of color, as Hilary tried to point out to her students. Sometimes yellow represented the light of God, and sometimes it just looked good against green.

Slowly the bus wound past the abandoned chapel on the hill for which Steeple Hill had been named. Hilary studied it for a moment. She glanced at the man in the seat ahead.

He was certainly very pale. With that tumbled hair and vaguely disheveled air he looked a cross between a street thug and a Romantic poet. His clothes were rumpled as though he had slept in them.

A fugitive and a vagabond . . . The Biblical reference somehow leapt to mind.

The bus hit a pothole and the fruit on the hat in front of Hilary bobbed wildly, temporarily blocking her view. Her next glimpse of the man ahead revealed him sitting up; from what she could see he appeared to be examining the contents of his wallet.

He made no effort at concealment. Hilary's dark brows drew together. His wallet was crammed with money, pristine green bills. Hundred dollar bills. He had to be carrying over a thousand dollars in cash.

The man began to count the money.

Hilary glanced at the surrounding passengers. Steeple Hill was a resort town as well as an artists' colony and it had its share of predators who fed off unwary tourists.

Oblivious to anyone's interest the man finished counting the money. Then slowly he counted it all again. When he had finished he stared down at it. Hilary could read the bewilderment on his features as though she had painted it herself.

He looked up. Following his gaze Hilary realized he was staring at the coin box where his crumpled note sat behind glass. She knew instinctively that if he could have recovered that bill without bringing further attention to himself, he would have.

The man slid the wallet back into his Levi's. As though he felt Hilary's gaze he glanced around. Hilary lowered her eyes, meditating on the brown knees beneath the cuff of her khaki shorts until it seemed safe to look again. Plastic fruit once more obscured her view.

The wail of sirens had everyone craning their heads, peering out windows as the bus swerved to the side of the road. A sheriff's car, blue and red lights flashing, streaked by, disappearing up the coast road. Seconds later another black and white flew past.

The bus resumed its journey. The passengers went back to talking and laughing—everyone but the man Hilary watched. He had not so much as glanced up as the police cars zoomed by. Hilary decided that was not a normal reaction.

The bus was now rolling into Steeple Hill, chugging up the steep, narrow streets past the gift shops, cafés and galleries, past renovated Victorian houses, flower boxes blooming in windows.

Lurching to a stop outside the iron gates of Fan Shell Park, the bus's doors flew open with a gust of exhaust. Everyone got to their feet, crowding out. Hilary stooped to retrieve her bag and sketchpad, edging out with the others.

The crowd from the bus rapidly dispersed into the larger crowd milling the sidewalk at four o'clock. The ocean air mingled with a variety of savory scents from the numerous restaurants lining the wharf. Distantly the bell from Steeple Hill chimed the hour. Only old timers like Hilary knew those silvery chimes were recorded and broadcast through loudspeakers strategically placed through-out the village. The bell in the chapel on the hill had been silent for many years; sold for scrap.

Hilary glanced around. There was no sign of the dark-haired man. She re-shouldered her knapsack and set off for home, deciding to cut through the park.

Just inside the tall iron gates a boy and girl with guitars sat singing a mournful ballad. Hilary recognized the melody of a hymn, though the duo sang of water too wide to cross over. The tune haunted Hilary's mind as she walked along the deserted path, her thoughts homing back to her work and her upcoming exhibition.

The long afternoon shadows stretched across the lawn like fingers. The perfume of the gardenia bushes lining the pathway scented

the stillness with their cloying sweetness. It was very still. Hilary's
sneakers on the hard-packed earth sounded un-naturally loud.

The hair on the back of Hilary's neck prickled. She had the
unpleasant sensation of being watched, but glancing around she
saw nothing unusual: trees, bushes, empty path. Though she wasn't
a nervous woman she found herself picking up her pace, breaking
into a half-jog, avoiding the tree roots across the uneven trail.

There was no sound of pursuit; just her feet slapping dirt, her
sketch book rustling the bushes. Feeling a little silly Hilary came
off the path on the other side of the park. With a sense of inevita-
bility she recognized the man sitting on the edge of the fountain
as the man from the bus.

Hilary checked and then continued on. Oblivious to her presence, the man sat, elbows braced on his knees, his head in his
hands.

She did not allow herself to hesitate. Walking up to the man,
Hilary placed a light hand on his shoulder. His shirt felt damp
from the spray of the fountain, and beneath it she could feel the
outline of hard muscle.

"Excuse me, are you all right?"

The man jumped as though he had been shot, gaining his feet
in a swift, healthy move he had looked incapable of making a moment before. Though Hilary was tall he seemed to tower over her.
His eyes, she noted taking a prudent step back, were a strange,
pale green. They gleamed in the pallor of his face like a startled
cat's.

"What?"

She saw then what she had missed before—or what had not
yet been visible—a bloody knot the size of a golf ball rose out of
his hairline.

"You're hurt."

The man seemed to gather his wits. Putting a hand to his
head he brought sticky fingers away, examining them curiously.
He offered a crooked grin which emphasized how weary and
unamused his eyes were.

"Just a flesh wound."

"Oh, you're English."

"British."

The attractive burr beneath those cultivated tones reminded Hilary of Sean Connery's James Bond.

His last reserve of energy spent, the man lowered himself once more to the fountain bench. He shut his eyes then widened them as though he was having trouble focusing.

"What happened? Is there someone I can call for you?" Hilary bent over him.

"I . . . don't think so." He answered as though it were an effort.

"Where are you staying?"

A pause. Then, "I'm not sure. I can't quite recall."

"You don't remember the name of the hotel?" Could he be concussed? Hilary wondered if he had been mugged? Then she remembered that wallet of cash. "That's easy enough. There are only four hotels here. We can call around and find out where you're registered."

"Where exactly is 'here'?" he cut in, fixing Hilary with that pale gaze.

"Steeple Hill." When his expression didn't change she prompted, "About half-way between San Francisco and Seattle. Northern California?"

"Calif—" His voice trailed off. He put a hand to his eyes, frowning fiercely. "I don't understand," he muttered.

"Look, let me get some help. You've got a bump on your head the size of my fist. There's a doctor's office around the—"

"No doctor," he interrupted.

Hilary paused. "Okay. That's up to you. I do think you might have a concussion. The pupils of your eyes don't look quite right."

Behind his hand the man gave a short laugh.

Pinching her lip, Hilary reconsidered. "Well, let's figure out where you're staying. There's a phone booth right over there." She nodded towards the red, European booth behind the trees.

No answer.

Unobtrusively Hilary checked her watch. Above the musical splish-splash of the fountain she could hear the ocean thundering beyond the houses lining the beachfront.

"It's no good phoning the hotels," the man said at last. "I don't know what name to give."

"You don't know?"

He raised his head. "I don't remember."

Hilary digested this in silence. She suggested simply, finally, "It'll be in your wallet, won't it?"

Green eyes met blue. Hilary knew the confusion she read was not characteristic of this man, whoever he was.

"There's no identification of any kind. Just money. Too much money," he muttered.

"How do you know it's too much money if you can't remember—?"

"There's nearly two thousand quid, if I've figured right."

Hilary remembered that a quid was the equivalent of the English pound. What was the exchange rate these days? "Maybe you're on vacation?" she offered. "Maybe you don't like traveler's checks?"

"What type of holidays do you go on, Miss . . .?"

"Jackson. Hilary Jackson." Hilary lowered herself on the bench beside him. The grainy cement felt warm against her bare legs though the salty evening air was cool. Nightfall came quickly by the sea.

"You're serious? You don't remember anything? Do you remember how you were hurt?"

Once more he leaned forward, head in his hands, hair curling between his splayed fingers. Hilary watched the slow rise and fall of his back as he took deep breaths, wondering if he was about to black out. Beyond the bruise there wasn't a scrap of color in his face.

"There was a note," he said at last. "A.X. Two o'clock."

"A note? Where?"

He didn't answer.

A.X. 2:00? Was A.X. a person or a place? Or for that matter a prescription? Take two Acebutolol Xylocaine? It was certainly cryptic. And four thousand dollars *was* an awful lot of loose change.

"What do you think the note means?"

Still no answer.

"Do those initials mean anything to you?"

"I believe it's an assignation," the man said at last.

Assignation? There was a good old-fashioned word right out of Agatha Christie. *Assignation in Abstract?*

"Do you think the initials are yours?"

"I don't know."

There was something despairing in those three words. Something that caught at Hilary's heart.

She mused aloud, "A.X . . . Albert? Alfred? Arthur?" She discarded those automatically. "Andrew? Do you think you would know your name if you heard it?"

"How should I know?" There was nothing despairing in that, and Hilary was faintly amused at her own reaction. Good Samaritan reflex? Or something more female?

"It seems to me that if you had a gut feeling—a response to a name . . ."

"What name?"

"Adam?" She liked the name Adam.

Nothing.

"Aaron? Abel? Abiah? Abner?"

"I'm glad you find this amusing, Miss Jackson," The voice behind his hands was edged.

Perhaps she was getting a little Old Testament. "Sorry. I am trying to help, really. I'm out of my area of expertise."

"As am I."

"If we knew your first name we'd have a starting point." Hilary considered more 'A' names. "Adrian? Alan?"

"Alan . . ." he repeated. He straightened. "Alan?" He rolled it off his tongue. Lines creased his forehead. "It is familiar. That may be it. Could it be Alan? Alan . . . but Alan what?"

Hilary watched him struggle with this for a few moments.

"Look," she said at last. "You're going to have to see a doctor. You may have fractured your skull. You've got to have x-rays."

"No."

"Memory loss is serious. Amnesia? Be realistic. Once you've seen a doctor we can contact the authorities. Someone may have reported you missing."

"Damn it, I said no!" The effort of arguing was taking more energy than he had to spare. He made an effort to control voice and face, and said placatingly, "Miss . . . Hilary, please believe me, I'm not badly hurt. I'd know if I were. Look at my eyes. Are the pupils uneven?"

Hilary stared into his eyes. Alan, if that was his name, gazed steadily back.

Beautiful eyes, remarked the painter in Hilary. Shape, color—that color was rare. She would like to paint those eyes. It occurred to Hilary that there was something uncomfortably personal, almost intimate about staring so deeply into a stranger's eyes.

"Black and dilated," she reported crisply to shake off that almost physical awareness. "You must know uneven pupils are not conclusive."

"They're conclusive if you have them," Alan retorted. "I'm not skull-fractured, just a bit dazed. If I could lie down for a bit . . . If I could just *think* . . ." That last bit was said to himself as though he had forgotten Hilary's presence.

Hilary did some thinking of her own.

"All right, listen, I live just down the road. If you think you can make it that far you can rest up there for an hour or two. I've got to teach a class at six-thirty but . . ." She didn't finish the thought aloud. The idea of leaving a stranger alone in her flat didn't thrill her, but he was injured and in need. She didn't see how she could turn her back on him.

Alan stared intently at Hilary. She had the impression that he was a man used to assessing people swiftly and accurately, but that suddenly he doubted his own judgment.

"You were on the bus, weren't you?"

"Yes." She gave Alan full marks for observation. She had thought him too preoccupied with his own aches and pains to notice his surroundings.

"Why?"

"I was working." She showed him her sketchbook, her knapsack. She smiled. "Why? Don't you trust me?"

"I don't trust anyone. I can't afford to."

"That's a strange thing to say." She spoke kindly. She did not say what she thought: what choice did he have? What choice did she have?

***

Hilary lived in the loft of a renovated warehouse not far from what had once been the Steeple Hill docks. She had lived there for nearly ten years, sharing the old brick building with the Thomas twins. The first floor, street level, was used by the Thomas's for their gift shop Two Deux. It had turned out to be a mutually ideal arrangement, and as the Thomas's owned the building there was no reason it shouldn't go on being an ideal arrangement for the next twenty years. Hilary anticipated no major changes in her life. Her father ruefully accused her of being the 'quintessential bachelor girl.'

Alan did the last leg of the narrow back staircase on sheer will power. His white face was bathed in perspiration and his eyes were slits of pain as he hauled himself, literally, up the last steps. His underbreath invocation was half-prayer and half-swear.

Offers of help had been brusquely declined.

The spirit that built the Empire, reflected Hilary. She watched Alan weave his way on to the top landing and lean into the wall, resting his head on his braced arm. His breathing echoed down the stairwell.

If he passes out, she promised herself, I'm calling the paramedics.

But he didn't pass out. He continued to stand there, sweating and panting, and Hilary unlocked the door and let him into the dark room, feeling for the light switch.

The overhead lights came on, mellow behind pastel fan-shaped shades, illuminating a long, wide room of white walls and shining hardwood floor. Four huge Palladian windows looked out over the ocean. Dark beams criss-crossed up into the open rafters high above.

There were paintings everywhere. Canvases on easels, canvases leaning against walls, against chairs, against a battered steamer trunk. Painted canvases, blank canvases. There was very little furniture: a red lacquered table and chairs, a giant painted screen at one end of the room, a bookcase at the other. A small, gilt-framed Monet hung over the ebony bookcase. This was genuine, given to Hilary by Grainger, her rep, in honor of her approaching thirtieth birthday. On the other end of the shelf sat a cheap plaster Rococo bust of the Virgin Mary. Hilary had bought this for two dollars in a yard sale moved by the way the artist had captured the yearning girl beneath the woman's strength.

Alan folded onto the nearest chair, his head dropping back, the bruise livid on his forehead.

Hilary dropped her painting gear and headed for the cubbyhole of her kitchen. She found the first aid kit in a drawer by the sink. She filled a metal bowl with ice, grabbed a clean dishtowel and returned to Alan, pulling a chair up next to his.

"Hey."

Alan opened his eyes and lifted his head as gingerly as though it were made of blown glass.

"Hey," he said thickly.

"I'm just going to try and . . ." Hilary suggestively dabbed the air with the wet cloth. "Unless you'd rather?"

He made no answer and Hilary reached forward and cautiously wiped at the stickiness matting his dark hair.

Alan sucked in his breath.

"Sorry."

"No. Go ahead." He clenched his jaw.

"I've never seen a lump this size on anyone's head," she

sympathized. "Outside of a cartoon that is. At least it hasn't bled much."

"Mm." He seemed to be focusing on her mouth. It made Hilary a little self-conscious. She was absurdly aware of his light breath against her face, the texture of his skin and hair beneath her fingertips.

"Almost done now."

"Marvelous."

"I'll wrap some ice in a towel for you. It should take down the swelling."

He grunted acknowledgment.

Hilary closed the first-aid kit. Setting aside the bowl, she rose. "You can lie down on the bed if you like."

His eyes shot open. "Haven't you a sofa?"

"Nope. Sorry. I'm not here a lot."

She felt his eyes on her until she disappeared behind the large Chinese screen at the far end of the loft which concealed her bed. It was an old iron monster she'd picked up for ten dollars at a yard sale. Hilary turned back the white goosedown comforter, plumped the pillows.

Alan stood up, hand to his head as though he feared it might fall off. Hilary watched him walk towards her. His eyes were half shut, his steps as cautious as a high-wire walker.

"All set," she assured him, moving aside in case he couldn't see her through the squint. He eased down on the mattress and sighed in relief. "Anything I can get you before I leave? Aspirin? Or maybe you shouldn't have aspirin. A hot drink? It's kind of chilly in here, I know."

His eyes opened. "Would a cup of tea be pressing my luck?"

"Of course not."

The glimmer of smile he offered was surprisingly charming. What was he like when he wasn't desperately weary, concussed and in trouble? Pretty devastating, Hilary guessed.

"Give me five minutes," she requested.

It took her closer to ten to wash off the sand and grime of the beach, and change into jeans and workshirt while the tea brewed. She was running late by the time she filled a towel with ice, poured the tea and carried it over to the bed.

The sight of Alan's lean length stretched out on her white blankets gave Hilary an odd fluttering sensation in her chest. Not exactly a Good Samaritan response, she thought wryly, setting the tea on the bed stand.

Alan sat up carefully and took the ice pack with a mutter of thanks.

"I'll be gone till about ten," Hilary informed him. "If you leave before I get back, will you lock up? Just turn the little button and shut the door. "

"Yes." He took a sip. His lashes lifted and he gave her a green, direct look. "Thank you. For everything."

"You're welcome. I hope everything works out for you."

Alan's lips curved in a caricature of a smile. "That makes two of us."

Hilary let herself out, quietly closing the apartment door.

She never expected to see Alan again.

***

There were books stacked on the bed-stand: C.S. Lewis's *Mere Christianity;* Josh McDowell; Max Lucado's *Just Like Jesus.* Her pillows smelled of paperwhites and sunshine. They smelt as she did. He closed his eyes, burying his face in the cool cotton. Instantly the staring eyes of the dead man sprang into his mind.

Christ, if he could just remember . . .

How could he not remember? It was like a nightmare. He kept thinking he would wake up. But wake up to what? If his bloody head would stop throbbing . . .

Throbbing? There was a polite word for the thunder of a thousand kettle drums rattling his skull. Well, he had been through worse. At least . . . he thought he had. Anyway the tea should help; caffeine would constrict the blood vessels in his head.

Honest-to-God brewed tea too, not that swill that passed for the real thing over here. That woman . . . What was her name? Panic surged. Then it came to him: Hilary. Hilary Jackson. It sounded British. He found that vaguely comforting.

She was a nice girl. Kind. Not his type, of course. What was his type? How could he know if a bird was his type when he didn't know his own name? But of course he knew. It was Alan. Alan . . . *was* Alan, right?

His thoughts shied away from this line of questioning as the thumps on the ceiling of his brain grew angrier, louder. Let it go. Relax. Think of something neutral. Think of—what was it? Hilary. Not his idea of a Jesus freak, despite the bedside reading selection. A painter, judging by this loft, those canvases. Practical though. Nice legs too. Not afraid to look you in the eye.

But could he trust her? The sudden doubt that transfixed him temporarily froze the pounding of his head. Did he know her? She seemed almost familiar. Was she somehow mixed up in all this?

All *what* for God's sake? What the hell was he involved in? Murder and God knew what else.

She couldn't be involved. Why should she help him? She couldn't have known he'd be on that bus. He hadn't known himself till the last minute. If she were in on it would she leave him alone here? Think it through. If only the bed would stop spinning long enough to let him think . . .

CHAPTER TWO

"Serena?"

Hilary paused, one foot on the bottom step of the staircase.

The woman poking her head out of the apartment doorway was several years older than Hilary. She was small and slender with a mane of curling brown hair and striking amber eyes. Her mouth was painted an uncompromising red. She wore jeans, a black T-shirt and a frown, which reversed itself.

"Oh, it's you. I thought you were Serena." Selena Thomas smothered a yawn. "What time is it anyway?"

"About a quarter to eleven."

Selena peered blearily at her watch. "You haven't seen my sister by any chance?"

"Nope. Sorry." Hilary smiled, trying to edge away up the stairs.

"Is it raining?" Selena's eyes took in the sparkle on Hilary's hair, the damp spots on the shoulder of her denim jacket.

"Not really. Just a mist."

Selena nodded absently, not really listening. She stepped into the hall, closing the door behind her. "Um . . . Hil . . . have you noticed anything strange about Serena lately?"

Weary, Hilary's heart sank as she read Selena's intent to keep her company. "'Strange' how?"

"Just . . . not her usual self," Selena hedged. "Secretive. She keeps doing this."

"Doing what?"

"Taking off at all hours, not letting me know where she's going."

"I haven't seen much of Serena lately," Hilary admitted.

They reached the top landing. All was quiet on the other side of Hilary's door. She fished her key out and inserted it in the lock.

Is he here or is he Memorex? she wondered as metal scraped on metal.

"It's probably some man," Selena grumbled. "Isn't there always a man involved? But why make such a mystery of it?"

Hilary opened the door to her loft. Across the room she could see her image mirrored in the picture windows: a tall, slender woman with cropped black hair, stars and mist shining through her reflection.

Alan sat at the table, one booted foot casually propped on the opposite chair as he pored over the map spread out before him. A mug of tea steamed at his elbow. Hilary had the impression he had been so immersed in the map that he had barely registered the sounds of their arrival. His instinctive turn, while not precisely guilty, seemed more wary than it should have.

"Speaking of men," Selena murmured. "I didn't realize you had company." Her amber eyes darted to the mussed bed at the far end of the room.

Oh lordy, Hilary thought.

"This is Alan," she introduced. "Alan, this is my landlord and good friend, Selena Thomas."

Alan was on his feet in one of those lithe moves that belied his battered appearance.

"Wow, what happened to you?" Selena commented, offering her hand. "You look like you've been through the wars."

"Believe it or not I fell down a flight of stairs." He said it with just the right touch of rueful candor so that Hilary opened her mouth to exclaim he'd got his memory—till she caught his eye.

Selena gasped, "Not our stairs, I hope?"

"Oh no." Alan offered an appealing smile, effective despite the bruises. Certainly Selena noticed the appeal and not the special-effects look.

"You're English, aren't you?"

"British."

"There's a difference?" Selena turned to Hilary, teasing, "So where've you been hiding him?"

"Uh—Alan arrived this afternoon." Hilary didn't want to lie to her friend, but Alan's gaze fastened on her profile seemed to compel her.

"Make it a long visit," Selena invited. "It's about time we had some interesting men underfoot."

Alan accepted the compliment, if it could be called that, with another of those white smiles. Watching Selena melt in its warmth, Hilary missed Alan's response. She tuned back in for Selena's cheerful, "Ten years now, isn't it, Hilary? It's a quaint little village but we like it. Aside from the occasional dead body."

"*What?*" Both Hilary and Alan stared at Selena.

"Oh, didn't you hear? It was on the radio. They found a body in one of the summer houses up at Smuggler's Bay. Probably a vagrant."

Probably. And yet Hilary felt uneasy. The unease increased ten fold as she met Alan's stare. She turned to Selena. "Do they know what happened?"

Selena wrinkled her nose. "The announcer said the man's identity was being withheld."

"He didn't say whether it was an accident or . . . anything?"

"She. If the authorities know they're not saying. Why?"

"Just curious." Hilary tried to avoid looking at Alan. She was amazed Selena couldn't feel the tension in the room, couldn't pick up Alan's guarded stillness.

"You're the last person I'd suspect of such morbid curiosity! Not," Selena added for Alan's benefit, "that dead bodies are a normal thing around here. We're law abiding folk for the most part."

Apparently reading something in Hilary's expression she finished lamely, "Well, I should be going. Alan looks like he could used an early night. You haven't forgot about the party, I hope?"

At Hilary's blank expression Selena rolled her eyes. "The party? *Your* party. The big 3-0?" She looked past Hilary to Alan. "Must be a mental block, you think?"

"Doubtless."

"Hilary did mention the party to you?"

He said vaguely, "I seem to recall . . ."

Selena looked exasperated. "That's Hilary. Grainger's throwing a big B-day for her over at the gallery tomorrow evening. You do know Grainger?"

"Hilary's mentioned him," Alan returned politely.

"And we will be seeing you?"

Alan glanced at Hilary who had remained silent through this exchange. "I hope so."

"Great." Selena too glanced at Hilary before adding, "Nice to have met you, Alan."

"The pleasure was mine."

When Hilary had closed the door after Selena she leaned back against it, folding her arms in an unconsciously defensive position. She said nothing, waiting; the trick of silence caught Alan under his guard.

"You're assuming my accident had something to do with this vagrant turning up dead."

"If he is—was—a vagrant."

"What's your theory?"

"I don't have a theory," Hilary said patiently. "I only know that you walked up from the direction of Smuggler's Bay, that you appear to have been in a fight and that you're afraid to go to the police."

"Circumstantial."

Hilary's dark brows rose. "Not coincidental?"

Pale green eyes studied her for a moment. At last he said, "I'm not afraid to got to the police, Hilary; but I'd like to face them with something more than an unexplained two thousand quid and no recollection of the past twenty four hours. My encounters with the law have left me convinced that its imagination is limited."

"Then you do remember something?"

The lines of strain around Alan's mouth and eyes seemed pronounced. "Nothing definite. Impressions, flashes—it might be memory. It's distorted. Like a dream. In the dream everything makes sense, but when you try to examine it afterwards . . ."

"Sometimes what you see in a dream is a symbol for something else."

"I'm not dreaming."

"But you are concussed. These memories are bound to be confused."

Hilary was aiming to reassure Alan, but he didn't look reassured. He gazed down at the map once more.

"Tomorrow I'll try up the coast," he said to himself. "See if I remember anything. Perhaps something will click. Perhaps someone will remember me . . ." His voice trailed. There was a queer, faraway look in his eyes.

Something brushed against Hilary's heart like a cold shadow. She was reminded of her feeling of being watched in the park that afternoon.

"I must book a room somewhere." Alan's voice dragged with weariness. He leaned on his hands braced on either side of the map.

Hilary looked within herself. "Why don't you stay here tonight?" she heard herself suggest. Am I demented, she wondered?

Alan slanted her an odd look. "What will the neighbors say?"

So he had not been blind to Serena's reaction.

"Don't worry about that. I'm used to sleep-over guests. There's a futon in the closet and plenty of extra blankets."

In the sudden stillness Steeple Hill's bell tolled the half-hour. Nearly midnight, thought Hilary. The witching hour.

"You're some kind of religious painter?" He seemed to speak at random, as though he were stalling. She followed his gaze to a canvas portraying an old man reaching his hand out to a dove.

"I paint what interests me," Hilary said. It didn't seem the right moment to get into a discussion about theology.

Silence.

"Why should you do this?" The harshness in Alan's tone sent her nerves jumping.

"It's the way I was brought up."

"To bring home strange men?"

"Of course not." With more conviction she said, "To do unto others."

Alan's expression didn't change.

Hilary asked gently, "Does everyone have to have an angle?"

"Most people do."

"You should get out more, Alan. Meet some new people."

Alan reached out, tilted Hilary's chin up. She stood very still at this invasion of her personal space. She met his eyes steadily. He had long, strong fingers. Hilary could feel the steel in his touch. Something changed in Alan's face, softened.

The next instant he had released her and stepped back.

"Why don't you undress?" she suggested, relaxing. Then hearing the echo of her words—and watching the arc of Alan's eyebrows "What I mean is, get into bed and I'll throw your clothes in the laundry."

For the space of a heartbeat he didn't move. Then, slowly, Alan began undoing the buttons of his shirt. Hilary hastily headed for the other end of the loft.

She dug the futon out of the closet and swiftly made up a bed on the wooden floor, aware all the while of Alan's unfamiliar masculine presence. She offered the laundry basket and he balled up his shirt and tossed it in. Hilary tried not to stare. Most of the men she knew were tanned a cancer-defying brown; she had to admit there was a certain appeal in the marble-smooth planes of Alan's tautly muscled chest.

"Don't you feel a bit uncomfortable undressing on stage?" He gestured at the tall black windows.

"You can't see up here from the street. You'd have to be out on the ocean. Go on, give the fish a thrill." Hilary continued into the kitchen.

She could hear the slide of a zipper, rustling sounds, the clink of a metal belt buckle hitting the floor.

"All clear," he muttered. Hilary heard the whisper of bedclothes as she came around the counter. Alan was easing himself down on the futon as though he ached in every joint. He caught her eye and grinned that crooked half-grin.

***

She told herself it was Selena's news about the dead man that made her uncharacteristically jumpy walking down to the basement. After all, the warehouse was as safe as a fortress. Iron bars pulled across the glass door of the shop front. The rear exit was secured by a heavy deadbolt. But as Hilary went down the creaking stairs she felt as though something lurked just out of sight, listening to her footsteps. The overhead light threw macabre shadows against the dingy walls in a Caravaggio effect.

When she reached the basement Hilary was surprised to find the light already on. The door to the Thomas's workroom was closed. Behind it she could hear the murmur of voices.

Hilary set the laundry basket down, turned on the machine and began measuring soap. There was no reason the Thomas's shouldn't hold a midnight discussion in the basement if they wanted to.

Hilary eased down the lid on the washer and ran silently back up the stairs. She didn't want to chance any more awkward questions about Alan. When she let herself into the loft he was sound asleep on the futon, blankets wrapped mummy-style. Even in sleep his face had a guarded look.

Hilary locked the door, turned off the lights and crossed the room to undress and slip between the cool sheets.

***

He was dreaming.

He was back in the house at Smuggler's Bay and he was staring down into the dead man's eyes. That was the old wives' tale, that a murderer's image was retained in the retina of his victim. He was staring into the dead eyes trying to see himself, trying to remember what he looked like . . .

The dream changed. Now he was in an interrogation room. There were two other men in the room. Sitting across the scarred table was the dead man. His blue eyes burned with hatred. His mouth twisted up in a sneer as he spat out, "But the law's on my side, isn't it? Isn't it?"

That 'isn't it?' rolled through his brain like the echo in a cavern. In the dream he sprang to his feet, the table flying over as he went for the dead man's throat. The second man in the dream came sharply into focus. He was one of those big, bluff sergeant major types. The sergeant thrust between them, pronouncing in stentorian tones, "There now, sir, that won't solve anything . . ."

Drenched in perspiration, his heart racing like a locomotive, Alan opened his eyes.

Hilary knelt beside him in a pool of rosy light, like an aura. Her dark hair was ruffled, her gray-blue eyes shadowed by long lashes.

"How many fingers am I holding up?"

Alan peered at her hand. "Three." His voice came rustily. His heart slowed to the tempo of his head. Rather like having a hangover with none of the fun.

"Who's president?"

"Who cares?"

Hilary smiled faintly. "Do you remember my name?"

"Hilary. Hilary Jackson."

She was wearing one of those oversized T-shirts silk-screened with a swarm of black and lavender butterflies. Underneath the T-shirt she was naked. He could see the soft swell of her breasts beneath the thin material, glimpse smooth brown thighs disappearing under the folds. The persistent throb in Alan's head was joined by a throb in another region.

"Do you remember your name?"

He frowned, trying to think. "Alan."

She had a lovely smile, wide and warm. It lit her grave eyes. But he didn't need the halo effect of the lights to tell him this woman was off-limits.

"How's your head?"

He studied her for a moment. "Don't ask."

Hilary's brows drew together. "Would you like some Tylenol?"

"Have you anything stronger?" Morphine? A gun?

Hilary considered. "There's some codeine left from when I had my wisdom teeth out last month. But I'm not sure—"

"That should do the trick."

She was up and back in a flash with a tumbler of juice and two white tablets. Alan sat up and she nearly over-balanced, tipping back on her heels. He steadied her, hand on her arm, and took the glass.

Hilary remained motionless, absorbing the sensation of warm fingers against her skin. Alan tossed back the tablets and swallowed a mouthful of ice cold orange and pineapple juice. Thirstily he drained the glass and handed it over.

"Thanks, luv."

'Luv,' as he would no doubt address any female from his landlady to the local barmaid. Wasn't 'luv' the British equivalent of 'toots?'

Shaking her head at herself Hilary returned to her own bed.

***

By nature Hilary was an early riser. Normally she woke with the day's work already laid out in her mind. Sometimes she felt almost desperate with the knowledge that there could never be enough time for all that she burned to put on canvas.

Today she woke with the knowledge that a strange man was sleeping on her floor.

Hilary rolled out of bed, took a quick shower and dressed, one ear pricked for signs of life from the other side of the room. Alan was still sleeping like a man with nothing on his conscience when she walked through to the kitchen. Or a man, she reflected, who had had codeine.

Noiselessly she moved about the kitchen. She switched the tea kettle on and ran downstairs to get the newspaper.

Serena was opening the shop on the ground floor. Sea air rustled the signs in the window. "Happy birthday!" she called from the far side of a rack of T-shirts printed with Selena's designs.

"Thanks," Hilary returned. "I've got a beautiful morning for it."

Despite her smile, Serena's eyes across the room looked puffy and red. Serena was the younger twin. She designed jewelry.

It had taken Hilary a year before she had been able to tell the Thomases apart. Luckily they had definite differences in taste. Selena generally wore black and favored red, red lipstick; while Serena used kohl eye-pencils and preferred bright exotic prints.

Hilary paused in the doorway. "Everything okay?"

"Sure." Serena flashed her a quick smile. "Why not? See you tonight."

"Tonight," Hilary agreed.

Seeing Serena reminded her of the muffled discussion she had overheard at midnight in the basement, which reminded Hilary of the laundry she had left in the washer. She trotted downstairs and dumped the wash in the dryer.

While she waited for the load to finish drying she unrolled the newspaper, skimming over it. Her eyes caught the dark blurb at the bottom of the front page signifying a late breaking story.

Hilary's breath caught and she sank down on the wooden apple crate beside a stack of empty cardboard boxes.

SCOTLAND YARD INSPECTOR FOUND MURDERED blazoned the headline.

A puzzle worthy of the fictional detective Sherlock Holmes came to light yesterday when the body of Scotland Yard Inspector Sir Alexander Napier was discovered in an abandoned house in Smuggler's Bay. Local authorities declined to disclose case details, revealing only that Napier, in this country unofficially, appears to have been murdered.

Please see **SCOTLAND**, page 8

CHAPTER THREE

Hilary threw open the door to the loft. Alan stood silhouetted against the picture windows. His hair curled wetly from the shower. He wore a white towel around his waist and an expression of male consternation, which might have been funny under other circumstances.

Hilary was in no mood to see the lighter side. She tossed his still damp jeans and shirt across to him. Alan caught them automatically against his chest.

"Get dressed and go."

"What?"

"You have to leave. Now." *He that smiteth a man, so that he die, shall surely be put to death.* Even now, knowing what she did, Hilary felt that tug of attraction. Silly, considering how familiar she was with every anatomical inch of the nude male. Silly and possibly dangerous. "You killed him, didn't you?" *Thou art the man.*

Alan's face changed. Grew watchful. He didn't have to speak. Hilary knew that it was true.

"It's not what you think. It was an accident."

"Please don't lie." Hilary held up the newspaper.

Alan's eyes flicked to the paper and then back to Hilary's face. "Don't believe everything you read." He shook out his jeans, and Hilary automatically turned, uneasily watching out of the corner of her eye as he yanked them on, balancing first on one foot than the other.

"The police are calling it murder."

"It wasn't murder. It was self-defense."

"I thought it was an accident?"

"It *was* an accident. He tried to kill me. I swear to God that's the truth. We fought. He fell and hit his head on the edgestone of the hearth."

Hilary turned to face him. "Alan, he was a *cop*. He was a Scotland Yard inspector. Their Art Thefts expert. You seriously want me to believe that he tried to kill *you?*"

Alan zipped his jeans and put his hands on his narrow hips. "I'm telling you the truth. You can bloody well believe it or not. He tried to kill me. How do you think I came by this?" He pointed to his forehead, still gruesome in the daylight.

"How come you remember this but nothing else?"

"I don't know. I just do."

Hilary found his sincerity convincing. Because she wanted to believe him? "Are you staying that Napier was a bad cop?"

"I don't know. I won't lie to you. Don't you see: until I get my memory back, until I can piece together what actually happened, I can't go to the police."

Hilary was shaking her head, denying this. Alan said, "All right, there is more. I think—I believe that Napier and I have butted heads before."

"That's not reassuring."

"Would you prefer reassurance or the truth?"

Reading the indecision in Hilary's face, Alan said curtly, " I can't ask you to trust me, I do realize that. All I'm asking is that you don't go to the authorities for—say, twenty-four hours. That should give time enough to trace my movements. Or perhaps my memory will return."

Crooked Scotland Yard inspectors? Murder? Amnesia? It sounded pretty far-fetched. But would a cold-blooded murderer have stuck around here once Selena had warned him that the body was discovered? Would a cold-blooded murderer make up such a ridiculous story?

"What are you planning to do?"

Alan's shoulders relaxed. She realized how tensely he had waited on her response.

"Rent a car and drive up to Smuggler's Bay."

"They say criminals always return to the scene of their crime."

"Seeing the house again may jog my memory."

"You need ID and a credit card to rent a car," Hilary pointed out. She tossed the paper aside.

Alan watched her walk into the kitchen and pour tea into mugs. She moved well, at ease with her body. And why not? It was a nice body. He shrugged into his shirt, waiting for her to make up her mind as he did up the buttons.

"I don't own a car."

"I thought all Yanks had cars."

"Not this Yank."

He took the mug from her and swallowed a mouthful of tea. Very hot, very strong. As he liked it. He smiled tentatively. Hilary did not return the smile. She turned her mug, first one way, then the other.

At last she said, "Selena has a car. I could probably borrow it for the day." She pushed a plate with muffins his way. Alan took one, bit into it. Poppy seed. How very Californian. He chewed slowly, thinking.

"The charge would be accessory to murder," he commented at last, as though remarking on the fine weather.

"It is now, isn't it?"

"At this point you could present a convincing argument."

Hilary shrugged. "With me you're less likely to attract attention than you are on your own."

He took her point. On his own he stuck out like a sore thumb. A British subject without any identification, and who just happened to be Johnny on the spot when a Yard inspector turned up dead?

"Perhaps it's not a coincidence," Hilary was reflecting aloud. "Napier was Scotland Yard's resident art expert. That's what the paper said. And Steeple Hill is well-known in art circles. The Pauley galleries are prestigious. There could be a connection."

A connection. As she said it something flashed into his brain.

A country estate. A paneled room with red damask draperies and gilt-framed paintings. And something else. On the floor, the body of a man.

Even as the picture slid into his mind he was pushing it away. This was different from his memory of Napier. This was horror. This crumpled figure in its blue smoking jacket was the stuff of nightmares. Alan jerked away from the memory and came back to the present, sweat popping out on his forehead. He heard Hilary query,

"Did you hear what I said?"

"Sorry?"

"From this article it sounds like Napier was a kind of minor celebrity. He's credited with recovering Sargent's *The Misses Vickers* stolen from the Sheffield City Art Galleries in 1993. He was also instrumental in foiling an attempt on the Tate Gallery earlier this year."

"Marvelous," Alan commented bitterly. "A national hero." Unobtrusively he wiped his forearm across his brow.

Hilary glanced up. She folded the newspaper and wedged it between the teapot and the creamer. "I'll check with Selena about using the car."

***

Hilary did not know if Alan had a plan beyond getting to the 'crime scene.' He was not sharing it, in any case. Their initial stop was a drug store where Hilary picked up such manly essentials as shaving cream, toothbrush and sunglasses. As an afterthought she grabbed a straw safari hat off a bargain table, dim memories of disguises and Nancy Drew novels running through her brain.

Their next stop was The Gap, Hilary maneuvering the Renault through the crush of Saturday morning traffic. She didn't drive enough to be comfortable behind the wheel, and when she did need to rent a car to visit her father in Seattle it was automatic transmission.

Alan made no remark about her sudden stops and starts, but perhaps he expected women to drive like that, Hilary reflected as she pulled up under some shady trees.

Alan peeled off a couple of hundred dollar bills.

"What if these are marked?" Hilary questioned, one hand on the car door.

Impossible to read Alan's expression behind the shades.

"Why should they be?"

"I don't know. It's a lot of money."

"It's a pay-off," Alan informed her.

"A—?"

"Marked bills would lead straight back to whoever wanted Napier dead." Alan slouched down in the seat and put the straw hat over his face, the conversation closed.

Not sure she followed his reasoning, but chilled, Hilary climbed out of the car and made her way across a sidewalk already crowded at ten a.m. with sight-seers and street artists.

What am I doing? she asked herself, pushing unseeingly through racks of Indian print shirts. Alan's words indicated knowledge that someone was behind his own involvement in Napier's death. Yet he had insisted Napier's death was an accident. Didn't these two facts contradict each other? Either Napier's death had been unplanned, an accident, or it had been premeditated, murder.

One thing was certain, Alan had not accidentally run into a Scotland Yard inspector in a deserted house on the California coast. Whether in this country 'unofficially' or not, Napier had some reason for being in Smuggler's Bay. Ultimately that reason had gotten him killed.

Hilary selected a pair of stone-washed jeans, a couple of Henleys, a dress shirt for that evening, and a sweatshirt. It was funny, she thought, that Alan could remember his measurements and not his last name. One should be as intrinsic as the other, shouldn't it? Maybe this kind of selective amnesia was not physical?

Or maybe it was not real?

Hilary paid for her purchases and went into the sunlight and smells of the busy street.

***

The drive up the coast to Smuggler's bay was short and windy. For once Hilary was blind to the beauty of the countryside, her attention on the man beside her.

"I wish the newspaper had more information," she said. His silence made her a little uneasy.

Alan made a sound of concurrence.

"If we just knew something more about why Napier was here. If it really was unofficial. Maybe something personal brought him to Steeple Hill."

Now she had his attention. "Something between the two of us, do you mean?"

"Well . . . not necessarily. You're Eng—British. Anything personal could probably have been dealt with on your home ground."

Smuggler's Bay was a collection of expensive summer homes along a lonely stretch of road overlooking white cliffs and ocean. According to local legend the cliffs concealed caves where long-ago smugglers hid their ill-gotten gains. In the ten years that Hilary had lived at Steeple Hill more than one luckless kid had drowned after a fall from those treacherous hills.

"Where to?" Hilary asked as they slowly wound up through the pine trees. This early in the season most of the homes were still boarded up.

"Right along here." Alan leaned forward, face tense as he scanned the roadside. "Here. Pull over."

A paved drive led down from the road to a house just visible behind a stand of trees. They could see white gables just above the tree branches, the sparkling blue of the ocean beyond.

Hilary parked beside the road.

"Wait here," instructed Alan. "If anyone comes, look like a tourist."

"Whoa," said Hilary. "I'm coming with you."

"Certainly not."

It was kind of touching, his belief in instant obedience on just his say so. Hilary hated to shatter his faith.

"Certainly yes. Alan, it's one thing for me to take a chance on you. Knowing what I do, I have to take responsibility for anything that happens. Anything that you do."

"I hope you're joking."

"I'm not joking."

She clearly was not joking.

Alan's irritation showed in the tightness of his jaw as he bit out, "Look, luv, has it occurred to you that I may already be known to the police? My prints are all over this place."

"Yes, that has occurred to me."

"They may be looking for me. If you're found with me—"

Hilary climbed out of the car and started down the drive. Alan swore under his breath. Catching her, he grabbed her arm.

"Then keep your head down and do exactly as I tell you," he hissed.

Gee, just like in the movies. Hilary nodded.

Crouching low Alan razor-backed his way down the hillside, keeping to the sparse cover offered by bushes and trees. Following Alan's example, Hilary made her way more cautiously down the slope. Although she was sure footed and used to clambering over sea walls and hills, she wasn't used to running doubled over and not able to make a sound.

Once her foot slipped on some pine needles and she fell in a slithering slide of loose pebbles and dirt, somehow managing not to cry out. She caught herself with a fistful of drooping pine branch. She scrambled back out of sight. Alan, a yard or so down, shot her an exasperated look.

Hilary made a face at him. A moment she later she joined him behind some prickly shrub. From this vantage point they had a clear view of the house and grounds. Hilary swallowed hard.

Two sheriff cars and a dark rental sat in the drive. A pair of uniformed deputies stood talking nearby. The perimeter of the yard had been taped off in official yellow.

"Why in the name of God would you bring a purse with you?" Alan demanded inaudibly, staring.

"It's not a purse," Hilary whispered back indignantly. She unsnapped the flap of the drab olive bag, fished around and handed him a binocular case.

Alan's expression changed. For the first time he offered her a genuine smile with no trace of that calculated charm. If she hadn't already been wearing sunglasses, Hilary would have reached for them in that blinding light of approval.

Alan handed Hilary the empty case and put the binoculars up to his eyes, adjusting them. Hilary was silent as the minutes ticked by, feeling the warmth of the sun on her shoulders, listening to the soft sounds of Alan's breathing and the voices of men below. The air was sharp and crystal clear. Every sound carried.

Hilary, her shoulder grazing Alan's, felt him stiffen.

"Jesus," he breathed.

Following the direction of his binoculars she saw two men walk out the front door of the house. One wore the uniform and insignia of Sheriff. The other was taller, broader, older. He was dressed in a dark suit.

"Who is he?"

A slight shake of Alan's head. He was following the two men's silent conversation intently.

Hilary watched. The man in the suit made a gesture of farewell to the sheriff, crossing the drive towards the rental car. Alan cursed under his breath. He thrust the binoculars into Hilary's bag.

"Time to go." He grabbed the bag, and with his free hand hauled Hilary to her feet.

His urgency communicated itself to Hilary and she climbed fast, keeping close to cover. Alan was right behind her; she could hear his feet scrabbling on the loose pebbles and granite. It was harder going up the hill than down. Hilary found herself making like an anteater as she reached the rise. Nothing like the fear of arrest to eliminate self-consciousness.

Alan caught her up. Without a word he took the keys Hilary held ready, starting the engine smoothly as Hilary closed the car door.

She raised herself and pulled Alan's smashed straw hat out from under her. "This road doesn't go anywhere," she warned him as the Renault shot away from the shoulder of the road.

"No matter," Alan replied, eyes in the rearview. "We can't chance his overtaking us." He shifted expertly into the next gear.

Hilary tried to reshape Alan's hat. "Do you know him then?"

"He knows me."

Alan drove on in silence. At the crest of the hill he parked beneath the swaying pine trees and turned off the engine. He rolled down the window. The hum of bees filled the air; the scent of sage and pine mingled with dust.

"How is it that you know that man back there knows you, but you can't remember who he is?"

"He's Scotland Yard. I had a dream last night. He was in it. Napier as well."

"What happened in this dream?"

"Nothing."

"Nothing? You mean you don't remember?"

Alan took off his sunglasses and pinched the bridge of his nose. "I don't recall. I woke up."

"I can't help you if you won't—"

"It was a dream," Alan bit out. His eyes glittered green like broken glass. "I don't know that it's relevant. I don't know that this ever happened, but—in the dream I tried to—to throttle Al— Napier. The sergeant broke it up."

"You just called Napier 'Al,'" Hilary pointed out. "Maybe that was subconscious. Maybe you knew him personally? Maybe you worked with him? Maybe you're a cop as well?"

"What?"

"Is it impossible? You must do something for a living. You're involved in this thing somehow, and we've agreed that there has to be a connection between Steeple Hill and Napier's art background. Maybe you and Napier were working together?"

"No."

"Why not?"

"Because I couldn't stand the sod—" He swallowed the rest of it.

Hilary pointed out reasonably, "Because you didn't like the man doesn't mean you weren't on the same side."

"It was an interrogation room."

"Oh." Hilary thought this over. "You're one of the bad guys?"

The laugh Alan gave was devoid of humor. He drummed his long fingers nervously on the steering wheel.

"You're thinking you're a crook? What, like an art thief?" Hilary watched a muscle jump in Alan's jaw. "Do you believe that?"

An image slammed into his brain: stone walls, steel bars, shutting off air and sunlight . . .

"No!"

"No," Hilary agreed.

He realized they meant two entirely different things.

CHAPTER FOUR

"So what's our next move?" Hilary speared a bite of grilled salmon.

They had stopped for a late lunch at a roadside café. They sat on the back patio facing the wild gold hills across an empty stretch of highway. It was just after two o'clock and they had the open deck with its pink and white umbrellas and lonely view to themselves. Alan watched Hilary tucking away salmon and rice pilaf, his own appetite still MIA. It didn't help that he wasn't sure what 'their' next move was. He had trusted that seeing the house at Smuggler's Bay would kick-start some memories—and so it had, but not the right ones.

Not that Alan was about to admit this to Hilary. Though she had been of great help, he was undecided as to how far to trust her Christian charity. Do-gooders didn't impress him.

One advantage to her presence was that Hilary had not yet been connected to him; she could go where he could not. But that wouldn't last. The bus driver could make him. Tracing Ms. Jackson would be a matter of days at most.

Hilary washed the salmon down with a swallow of raspberry tea and Alan shuddered inwardly. Yanks! "Assuming unofficial business wouldn't get Napier killed, even though that was an accident, what kind of official business would bring him into this country?"

Alan leaned back into the floral cushions, swirling the liquid in his glass.

"Art," he said without hesitation. "Theft or fraud."

He had restless, beautiful hands. Not the hands of a laborer, Hilary decided. Not the hands of an artist either. What then? The hands of a gentleman? A gentleman thief?

"Something which began in Eng—Britain."

Alan nodded. "Something which connects Steeple Hill's art community."

"That doesn't exactly narrow the field."

"It must. Tell me this, why Steeple Hill? What does Steeple Hill have that no other place does?"

"Granny Annie's milk gravy and biscuits."

"You're joking, I imagine."

"Sorry. Well then, our artists."

"Quite. But why these particular artists? Why shouldn't any so-called art colony do?"

"I don't know. If it's something illegal, and I guess it has to be for Scotland Yard to be involved—"

"And big," Alan cut in. "Don't let's forget one doesn't drag the Yard in on every smash and grab job. This seems to be international, spanning your country and mine."

"Okay, so a lot of money must be involved," Hilary pursued his reasoning. "That means considerable risk must be involved."

Risk. Unconsciously he put his fingers to his forehead.

Hilary went on, "I guess you'd need to have artists, top-notch artists at that, who aren't afraid of taking chances."

"And who aren't suffering a surfeit of moral qualms."

"Well . . . right. You're not thinking of anything simple like . . . theft?"

"No."

"No. Because other artists are involved. If other artists are necessary then we must be looking at something like forgery." Hilary stared at Alan.

"Theft and forgery."

"But—"

"Pretty obvious, don't you think?"

What was obvious, Hilary thought uneasily, was that Steeple Hill's artistic community was a small and intimate one. If Alan's hypothesis was correct, someone Hilary knew, maybe a friend, was involved in art theft, forgery and possibly even murder.

Except that Sir Whatsit *hadn't* been murdered. His death had been an accident. Alan claimed Napier had been trying to murder *him*.

So what do we have?" Alan invited.

Hilary decided that that veddy veddy British accent just might get on her nerves. Especially when Alan took the tone of Holmes prompting Watson.

"You're suggesting that there is an international ring of art thieves and forgers based here in Steeple Hill?"

"Yes." He clipped off the word.

"That doesn't strike you as a little far-fetched?"

"No."

"No? Not only that, I don't see how this gets us any closer to proving to the police you didn't murder Inspector Napier."

"If I can prove a connection—"

"But how could an operation like that carry on here without anyone suspecting? Steeple Hill is a village. Everyone knows everyone else's business."

"It wouldn't have to be a large operation," Alan pointed out. "Merely tightly run."

"How in the world could we ever prove any of this? It's all guesswork. Unless you do remember something?"

Alan shook his head. "It is guesswork. But educated guess work."

"What makes you think so?"

He spread his hands. "I simply know. I know this is familiar territory."

"Great," muttered Hilary, "because it's the Twilight Zone to me."

Alan stared at her. "If this is getting too close to home, say the word."

"Is that British humor?" Hilary set down her fork. "You think I'm afraid of the truth?"

She did not strike him as a woman afraid of the truth. She also did not strike him as a woman who would concern herself with the criminal activities of her neighbors. Hilary seemed to have her own code of ethics.

Alan said slowly. "You don't know me. You don't owe me anything. You have loyalties—"

"Yes, I do," Hilary interrupted. "But I'm not worried about being true to this hypothetical thief and forger friend. I don't believe there's a ring of international art thieves in Steeple Hill, but maybe you're right and something sinister is going on. The thing is, you can't remember your own last name, you don't know what you were doing in that house, or even in this country, so I think your deductions, Mr. Holmes, are open to question."

"Fair enough," Alan said evenly.

"Let me ask you this: what makes you think the money in your wallet was a—a pay off?"

"The amount of cash, although I suppose it's small for a contract. A hit," he clarified.

"Like what, a Mafia hit?"

"I don't think the Mafia is involved."

"But you think someone paid money to kill a Scotland Yard detective?"

"The wallet was brand new, right down to the stick-on price tag. There was the note and the money. Let's say someone was adding incentive to the idea of getting rid of Napier."

"Maybe the wallet was Napier's?"

"Napier had his ID. That's how they identified him. Besides, why should Napier want to off *me*?" Alan was frowning as though this idea were in poor taste.

"But he did, didn't he? You said he was trying to kill you."

"Yes."

Hilary sighed. Alan didn't trust her. Did she trust Alan? She was risking a lot for a man who might be as bad as he feared.

As though reading her mind, Alan demanded, "I still don't understand. Why are you helping me?"

Hilary smiled faintly. "Are you a Christian?"

"I don't . . . I suppose so. I'm not sure what you mean."

THE ART OF DYING

It was amazing how that question could fluster or antagonize. "Do you believe in the teachings of Jesus, the Christ?"

Alan looked uncomfortable. "I suppose."

"That's the difference between us. I don't suppose, I believe. I live every day as close in accordance with the teachings of Christ as I can."

Alan blinked. "You're helping me because it's the Christian thing to do?"

Hilary grinned. "What did you think? Love at first sight?"

"Frankly neither one's easy to believe."

"Oh ye of little faith."

He scowled. "I can't tell if you're serious or not."

Hilary shrugged, toyed with her fork. "All right, let me ask you this. Do you trust your instinct?"

"Yes."

Hilary said nothing, waiting. Alan protested, "Hilary, I don't even know if I'm married."

That won a laugh out of her. "Alan, I'm not proposing!"

Disconcerted utterly, Alan tried to get the conversation back under his control. "Fine. I accept your help. Tell me about some of your fellow artists."

"You can check them out for yourself tonight. The party, remember? At the gallery."

"*The* gallery? There's only one?"

"There's only one real gallery in Steeple Hill. The Pauley."

"The Pauley? I thought that was in New York."

Now that's interesting, Hilary noted. How many people not in the biz would know where the Tate was located or The Whitney? Yet Alan, who was English yet, knew where the Pauley was located.

"One here and one in New York," she replied. "Owned by Grainger Pauley."

"The same Pauley who handles your work?"

"Bingo."

Alan made no comment to this. He drained his glass and

reflected aloud, "I wonder if the local lads will risk offending the *beau monde* by showing up tonight?"

"Showing up tonight? The *police?*"

Her tone seemed to amuse him. "Certainly. Do you imagine your sheriff's department can't reason as quickly as we've done? They're privy to information we lack. Whatever Napier's sergeant knows, they know."

Hilary had trouble picturing the local sheriff's department unraveling a complicated plot of art theft and forgery. Homicide yes, but this wasn't a simple matter of a barroom brawl or domestic violence. This was the stuff of which Lifetime Channel movies are made.

"But the papers said Napier wasn't here officially."

"That means only that he hadn't checked in yet with the local boys. Either he wasn't in this country long enough or he didn't want interference."

Possibly not, if he was planning to kill Alan in an abandoned house.

"What happens if the police show up tonight?"

Alan shrugged this off as no big deal. "I don't suppose they will. They've enough on their plate with tracking Napier's movements and the postmortem results."

Postmortem. Autopsy. Feeling sick, Hilary laid down her fork.

Alan was immediately on his feet. "Finished? Let's roll out."

They were winding their way through the empty tables. A bus boy noisily clearing dishes when Alan checked mid-step. He stared and stared. Then Hilary watched him remove an empty matchbook from one of the dirty table's ashtray and slip it in his pocket.

"What's up with the matchbook?" she asked once they were back in the car.

Alan handed over the white matchbook. Hilary turned it, examining the silver crest.

"The Seven Palms Hotel in San Francisco?"

"I remember seeing this before," Alan told her with suppressed excitement. "I recognize this crest."

"It must mean your memory's coming back!"

"It means we've got our first genuine lead. Tomorrow we'll check out this hotel and see what we turn up."

"Maybe you were staying there?"

"Possibly." Alan studied the matchbook cover as though it held the secrets of the universe.

"We could start for Frisco now," Hilary offered. She could see him weigh it, then reluctantly give up the idea.

"No. We wouldn't make it back in time for your party." And then, lest she think he was concerned with her birthday plans, "We're not likely to have all these people so conveniently assembled again."

***

"You were saying?"

Alan turned from the ceiling-high window in Hilary's loft with its view of fiery, phosphorous sunset, and gave a low whistle.

Across the room Hilary was rummaging in a trunk. She shook the folds out of a black lace shawl, and glanced at him inquiringly. This was a Hilary unlike any Hilary he had met before. Her black, cropped hair was sleeked back from her face, dramatically accentuating her bone structure. Bronze lipstick played up a sexy mouth, gold shadowed wide cheek bones and sensuous eyes. The black dress Hilary wore was a very simple, but Alan recognized , very chic little number which hugged her curves and left her brown shoulders bare. Her only ornament was a pair of large, gold Celtic earrings.

"What was I saying?" Alan knew he sounded vague. Originally he had thought this woman plain. Nice legs, pretty eyes. She was riveting.

"You were saying the stereotypical rich, mad art connoisseur is a myth."

"Right." Alan was relieved to focus on business. "Typically the people buying stolen paintings are unsuspecting collectors, more often than not Yanks. You people ask more questions buying an automobile than a purported Old Master. But of course there's the exception to every rule. An occasional work will be stolen to order for a connoisseur, but most art thieves aren't specialists."

"The art market took a nose dive last year. Times must be tough for art thieves along with everyone else."

"Exactly. By the same token the stakes are higher. In Europe art theft is growing faster than any other form of larceny."

"So," Hilary said slowly, "Looking at this from a business standpoint, probably the biggest asset to a thief would be a reliable distributor. Someone who either finds the buyers ahead of time or can market stolen paintings to collectors who aren't going to ask too many questions."

"A gallery."

"No. A legitimate gallery would never involve itself in fraud or theft."

"Think out of the frame for a moment. Who is in better position to market stolen art?"

"But not a real gallery. Not a big gallery," Hilary objected. "A reputable gallery like the Pauley isn't going to risk everything trying to move questionable paintings."

Alan looked unconvinced.

Hilary glanced at the clock on the bookshelf. "We'll be late if we don't leave now. Anyway, you'll see what I mean."

***

Although the gallery was within walking distance, Hilary had arranged to drive with Selena and Serena. She and Alan folded themselves into the back seat of the Renault, thighs brushing, shoulders touching. The car interior was rife with the mix of perfumes. Alan cracked the window.

"What part of England are you from, Alan?" Selena asked from the front seat. The younger twin, Serena was driving.

Alan snapped out of trying to tell the Thomases apart. "London," he answered off the top of his head. That felt right though. He had a quick dizzying mental slide show of fog on the Thames, red double-decker buses, Victoria Street, the Old Bailey . . . barristers in powdered wigs . . .

"Will you be staying long?" That was the other one, Serena, her eyes pinned on the traffic ahead of them.

"Not long." He became aware of the warmth of Hilary's body pressed against his own. Oddly, it centered him.

"Alan dropped in for my birthday," Hilary put in. "I'm trying to talk him into spending the week."

"You arrived on Friday?" Selena inquired.

"That's right."

It seemed to Alan that something had changed in Selena's manner towards him. He felt a chill he had not felt before. Her questions were more pointed.

"What is it you do, Alan?" she asked now, turning her head to look at him.

"I'm a . . ."

It was like stepping down on the sawed-thru rung of a ladder. One instant the answer was solid beneath his feet, the next there was thin air.

"Alan is an insurance salesman," He heard Hilary answer without missing a beat.

"You're kidding!" the sisters cried in unison.

Alan stared out the window, afraid his expression would give him away to Selena's tawny gaze.

"Nope, really," Hilary lied blithely, and patted his knee.

***

In the dusk the Pauley Gallery looked like a UFO crash-landed amidst the gingerbread Victorians: white cantilevered curves, geometric overhangs, tinted sheets of windows like giant mirrors stood in stark contrast to the Old World ambiance of Steeple Hill.

The Renault pulled up at the crowded curb and the four of them piled out.

"Pretty little thing, isn't it?" Selena quipped following Alan's gaze.

The sisters vanished through the open doorway. Alan held Hilary back for a moment.

"Insurance salesman?"

Hilary gurgled with laughter. "Think about it; people will spill their life stories in an effort to head off your sales pitch."

***

Grainger Pauley met them at the door; the king welcoming the crown princess.

"Hilary, my pet. Happy birthday." He took her hands and kissed both of her cheeks before turning unhurriedly to Alan.

As Hilary performed the introductions she was aware of two supremely confident males sizing each other up.

Grainger was about fifty-five though he could still pass for ten years younger. He was tall and tanned and fit. His hair was dyed gold, but so expertly he could still deny it. His eyes were blue and canny, raking over Alan's tall figure.

"Well, well," Grainger said slowly, shaking hands with the younger man.

"Well, well what?" Hilary questioned. Grainger seemed to be giving Alan a mighty close going over for someone not in the market.

Feeling Hilary's gaze, Grainger's eyes found hers. His smile was unrevealing. "Selena mentioned you were bringing an old friend by. I don't believe we've met before, have we?" he asked Alan.

"I don't believe so."

"You seem familiar somehow."

Hilary's heart skipped a beat. Alan said coolly, "I have one of those faces."

"You do, don't you?" Grainger smiled a perfunct smile and gestured to the spacious room. Guests with brimming glasses milled around several enormous sculptures. On a trestle sat a gigantic

cake like still another sculpture. A white-jacketed caterer paused
with a tray of fluted champagne glasses.

Hilary and Alan each took a glass.

"Drink up. Enjoy," urged Grainger. "You only live once." He
patted Hilary's cheek sharply. She opened her mouth but Grainger
was already off on his hostly rounds.

Hilary murmured, "That was odd." Her eyes followed
Grainger's figure as he mingled in the press of people.

"How so?"

"Just the way he reacted to you. Almost . . ." Hilary couldn't
put her finger on it. 'Hostile' was too strong a word.

"He fancies you," Alan remarked.

The very idea made Hilary uncomfortable. "He likes me, sure,
but Grainger is first and foremost a business man. I'm an investment
to him."

Alan swallowed champagne noncommittally.

"Maybe he recognized you?"

"No, I didn't pick that up."

"What are you two whispering about?" Selena rejoined them,
caviar-smeared cracker in one hand, champagne glass in the other.
Alan knew it was Selena and not the other bird because this one
was a shade or two paler, her hair darker. She favored bright red
lipstick. The younger sister, Serena, emphasized titled eyes with
Egyptian style eyeliner. Her brown mane was sun-streaked, or at
least treated to look that way.

"Hilary's briefing me," Alan informed Selena.

"How boring for you." Selena offered Hilary a bit of caviar on
cracker. Alan watched Hilary bite in and make a slight face. Her
tongue flicked out to retrieve an errant crumb.

Selena was smiling faintly, watching. Feeling Alan's gaze she
asked, "How's your head?"

There was something hard in her eyes as they met his own,
almost challenging.

"I hardly know it's there," he assured her.

Hilary chuckled. Selena's smile was polite.

"You said you fell down a flight of stairs?"

"That's right."

"You're lucky you didn't break your neck."

"I generally land on my feet."

"Not always." Selena's glance rested on his bruised face.

"No not always."

"But then you're probably covered under one of your own life insurance policies."

Hilary begged, "Don't get him started."

"I'm a fanatic when it comes to work," Alan agreed.

Hilary and Selena appeared to have a friendship of long-standing. It appeared also to Alan that there was some undercurrent running through this intimate gathering of Hilary's friends and colleagues. It might not have anything to do with the murder of a foreign policeman. It might be the reaction of a clique to an outsider. Then again, it might be something more sinister.

"Well, that's one thing you have in common," Selena commented. "I'm convinced Hilary leaps out of bed in the morning with the flame of inspiration blazing in her eye."

"And you thought it was lust," Hilary chided Alan.

Selena laughed.

"What's so funny?"

They turned to face the newcomer, a slight young man with long red hair and a Vandyke beard.

"Hi, Bry," Selena greeted unenthusiastically before flitting away.

Hilary introduced Alan to Bryan Kinsale. Bryan's handshake, like everything else about him, was too intense.

"So," he said maliciously, brown eyes trained on Hilary. "No more of the child prodigy stuff, eh? The big 3-0. Middle age."

Hilary smiled politely and hid behind her champagne glass. Catching Alan's curious gaze, Bryan bit out, "From Bible stories to The Whitney in one easy lesson. MOMA? The Met? What were you, Hil, twenty-five?"

"I'm the first person to agree that I've been blessed, Bryan."

Bryan's face screwed up as though in pain. "That's right. She's the Chosen One." He stared at Alan. "Don't tell me you don't *know?*"

"Of course he knows."

"He doesn't look like he knows."

"That's what you call a well-schooled expression."

"That's what I call faking it."

"Don't mind me," said Alan.

Bryan sized up Alan. "Want to model for me?" he demanded belligerently.

Hilary choked on her champagne as Alan replied, "Why not?"

"When?" Bryan demanded. "Tomorrow?"

"We'll call you," Hilary said firmly. "Would you excuse us, Bry? I want Alan to meet someone." She tugged Alan's elbow.

Bryan guzzled the dregs of what was clearly not his first glass of champagne, sneering, "Sure, play the game. But art's not about social values and bourgeois hang ups . . ."

"No no no," Hilary was murmuring to Alan. "You don't want to spend time naked with Bryan. Not in your physically weakened condition."

Alan looked amused. "I think spending time with Kinsale might prove informative."

"Oh it would, but Bryan's not involved in any art ring. No one would trust him. He's too unstable." They paused in front of a towering black obelisk as though Hilary were showing it to Alan.

"How unstable?" He matched her undervoiced tones.

"For one thing he's bitter about Grainger's refusal to handle his work."

"Is his work good enough?"

"Yes, but Grainger says it's not commercial. I think he means Bryan is not commercial."

"Is that Pauley's criterion?"

"Like I said, Grainger is a businessman. Art is his business."

Alan said suddenly, "You're not like any church-going girl I ever met."

Hilary grimaced. "I know. I try though."

He didn't know what to make of that. He hadn't been criticizing her; he just couldn't figure her out.

Undervoiced, Hilary said, "Never mind that now. Let me introduce you to our next suspect."

Rebecca Nash was a sculptress and she looked the part in a flowing red caftan, her gray hair bobbed, her powerful hands adorned by heavy, silver jewelry. She was about sixty and her deeply tanned face was livened by laugh-lines and twinkling hazel eyes.

"Becca's one of Steeple Hill's institutions," Hilary informed Alan when introductions had been made.

"That's right." Becca winked at Alan. "I was suffering for my art when Hilary's bedroom was still being used to smoke fish."

If she had been a starving artist, those days were long past.

"You must know Steeple Hill inside out," Alan remarked, going to work with that deliberate charm Hilary recognized. Even his voice changed, she thought. Became smoother, more confidential. Maybe insurance *was* his calling.

Becca smiled good-humoredly. "Maybe I remember a few things our town fathers would just as soon I forget."

"Not many secrets in a small town, I imagine?"

"As far as that goes," Becca remarked, "I'm sure we all have our little secrets." She raised one painted brow meaningfully at Hilary.

"Becca, you and Grainger started out together, didn't you?" Hilary put in. "Before Grainger gave up painting?"

"Grainger and I go way back," Becca agreed. "Thick as thieves." Her smile was a little less free as she raised her glass.

"Hilary?"

Hilary started guiltily. Grainger looked amused at her reaction.

"Telling tales, Becca?"

Becca raised her champagne glass. "Cheers."

"Forgive me," Grainger said, "but may I borrow you for a few minutes, my pet?"

"Yes, of course."

Hilary handed her glass to Alan and walked away with Grainger. He led her straight to his office, a leather-lined inner sanctum complete with silver-framed photos of Grainger with art world celebrities. There was a Rauschenberg on one wall and a framed pencil sketch of Grainger on a paper napkin that Hilary had done ten years ago at their first meeting.

For the first time in the years she had known Grainger, Hilary sensed he was uncomfortable. He took his time lighting one of his expensive cigars. She consciously uncurled her hands, breathed quietly.

"I had a visit from the police today," Grainger said.

Hilary couldn't help the gasp that escaped. Grainger looked up.

"Yes, I was surprised myself."

"Why?" she asked. "Was it something to do with that murder in the papers?" Was that a normal conclusion to jump to?

Grainger puffed away. 'I'm sure the murder was behind it," he admitted finally, "but that's not what the Sheriff was asking about."

"What was he asking about?"

"Don't ask 'what.' Ask whom," Grainger informed her without a trace of his usual good humor.

"Whom was he asking about?"

"About you, my pet," Grainger answered bluntly. "All about you."

CHAPTER FIVE

"I don't recollect Hilary ever mentioning your name before, Alan," Becca was saying.

Alan tore his eyes away from the last glimpse of Hilary's slim, black-clad figure disappearing into a side door. Meeting alert hazel eyes he warned himself that this lady didn't miss much.

He put his hand over his heart. "I'm wounded."

Becca chuckled obligingly but persisted. "You're old friends, I think Hilary said?"

"We lost touch over the years, Hilary and I," Alan replied. This was the story he and Hilary had agreed on earlier. "We're getting to know each other all over again."

"I see."

"I'd no idea she'd become so successful."

"Then you're not involved in the art world yourself?"

"I'm an insurance salesman."

Becca swallowed champagne the wrong way but made a gallant recovery.

"How . . . interesting. Would you like to see some of Hilary's work?"

"Love to."

Smiling inwardly Alan let Rebecca Nash lead him upstairs.

Clearly familiar with the upper echelons of the gallery, she guided him up another flight of stairs and down an unlit hallway.

The overheads switched on, revealing a long, airy room lined with paintings.

"Everything you need to know about Hilary but were afraid to ask," Becca said with a wide gesture, leading the way.

Curiously Alan studied the nearest painting. The technique

was traditional yet startling. Sails billowed against slate skies, the hull of glistening malachite and bronze cut through the ultramarine waters: Peter on the White Sea. Simple, so simple, yet the subtle mood of the thing shattered his cynicism.

Two things struck Alan. The first was that Hilary Jackson was a formidable talent. Talent? An insipid word for what was truly a genius. The second realization was that he knew a helluva lot about art. Perspective, composition, brush technique, properties of color, properties of light . . .

"Is it all Christian-themed?"

"Mostly." Becca eyed him curiously. "Wasn't it before?"

"Before what?"

"When you knew her?"

"I suppose so," he said, his tone purposely vague. He walked towards another painting.

"It doesn't matter what she paints really. She's going to be recognized as one of the Masters of our century," Becca said without emotion beside him. It was fact. Pure and simple.

Rebecca moved on. "The Getty is negotiating for this one."

Alan followed Rebecca down the wall of paintings. He stopped and stared. Shimmering hills of gold, achingly blue sky, a robed woman running with her arms outstretched like a child.

There was a roaring like the wind in Alan's ears and the floor rushed up to meet him.

"Alan, my dear boy! *Alan!*"

From a long way off Alan heard Rebecca Nash calling to him. He became aware that her unexpectedly strong arms were the only thing holding him up. He was weak as water, sick and shaking.

"Alan . . ."

He could hear the alarm and bewilderment in Becca's voice. He made a supreme effort to get control of himself. It was all he could do to stumble with her help over to a Formica bench. He bent forward putting his head between his knees. His face was cold with sweat and there was a ringing in his ears.

Rebecca's insect voice told him to take deep breaths. He obeyed.

Pictures flashed through his brain. A woman's face, a peasant face full of comfortable sensuality; Rembrandt's Hendrickje as Ruth, dissolving into burnt-gold hills, and at the very foot of the hills, a no-nonsense signature: Hilary Jackson.

Nausea threatened to overwhelm him. Rembrandt? The California hills? Hilary's signature? What could these things have to do with each other? He heard his breathing, quick and harsh in his ears. He focused on that and the chaotic images in his brain receded. The ringing in his ears faded.

"Stay put," Becca instructed. "I'll get Hilary."

Alan sat up. "No, I'm all right."

But Becca was halfway down the hallway, her heels echoing on the polished floor.

***

"*Me?*"

Hilary stared at Grainger. "I don't understand."

Grainger shrugged. "Perhaps I do. Tell me about this new friend of yours. Alan. Alan—what?"

"Alan . . . Allen," Hilary said lamely. "But I've known him for years."

"You've never mentioned him before, my pet."

"Grainger, I haven't told you about every man I ever knew."

"Of course not." Grainger made soothing motions. "But after all there haven't been so many of them in the ten years we've known each other."

"I suppose not."

"Your beaus were all artists; so it was natural that I would know them, whereas Selena tells me Alan sells—er—insurance."

"Yes."

"Not that there's anything wrong with that, my pet. You don't have to make apologies for him."

"I wasn't going to." A little exasperated, Hilary said, "Grainger, I did have a life before I came to Steeple Hill."

"Of course you did." Grainger sounded unconvinced. "I suppose you met this fellow when you were in England. When was that?"

"When I was eighteen."

"That's right. You were on a Mission or something."

"No, I was on a walking tour with friends."

"That's right."

Hilary couldn't tell if Grainger was buying this or not. His eyes never seemed to leave her face. "And you met this Alan then? Twelve years ago?"

Be sure your sin will find you out. "Yes."

"And he—Alan—turned up here exactly when?"

"Friday."

"Friday morning? Friday night?"

Hilary decided to turn and fight. "Why the catechism, Grainger?"

"Catechism? I thought this was conversation. A private conversation between friends. Between partners."

Hilary did not speak.

"After all, your father is in Seattle. I suppose I feel some responsibility . . ."

"Oh please."

Grainger stubbed his cigar out. "Very well, my pet, let's be frank. I'm concerned that there might be some connection between this mysterious young man of yours and that murder at Smuggler's Bay. I think perhaps that's what the police were hinting."

"That's ridiculous."

"Is it?"

"There's nothing mysterious about Alan." Hilary thought rapidly. "Alan is English. So was that policeman. That's the only connection I can think of. What did you tell the police?"

"I didn't tell them anything," Grainger said regretfully. "I didn't know till this evening that you even knew this man."

That's not true, Hilary thought. You weren't surprised to meet Alan.

Why should Grainger lie?

Someone rapped on the office door. Rebecca Nash poked her silver head into the room.

"Hilary, you'd better run upstairs. Alan's ill."

Hilary took the stairs as swiftly as the short, narrow skirt of her dress would allow. Becca's voice floated behind as she climbed more slowly, Grainger in tow, "He was standing there staring at one of Hilary's paintings when he keeled over. Head injuries are tricky things. Do you think it could be some kind of delayed reaction?"

"Which painting was he looking at?" Grainger inquired, as though this were the only point of interest.

Hilary rounded a bend in the staircase and nearly crashed into Alan. He steadied her, hands warm on her bare shoulders.

"Becca said you were ill," she said staring. He looked pale but perfectly normal.

Alan's brows rose. "I felt lightheaded for a minute, that's all."

"Lightheaded!" expostulated Becca catching them up. "My dear, Alan, you'd have been kissing the carpet if I hadn't been there. You're still white as a sheet."

"Naturally fair-skinned," Alan assured her.

Plainly Alan didn't want attention drawn to his moment of weakness. Hilary tried to hold up her end. "I know my paintings are good, darling, but I'd no idea they were that good."

Alan's laugh sounded completely natural. He draped his arm around Hilary's shoulders as they proceeded downstairs. Becca and Grainger moved aside.

Hilary heard Grainger mutter something solicitous to Becca who grumbled, "Don't I know it. It's not getting old I mind. It's the side-effects."

"Did you want to leave?" Hilary asked Alan low-voiced as they reached the ground floor where the party continued in full swing.

Alan's smile should have convinced anyone watching. "Things are just getting interesting."

"I'll say. Grainger said the police were here today asking questions about me."

Not by the twitch of an eyelash did Alan indicate he found this news disturbing. "All the more reason not to bail. What did Pauley tell them?"

"Nothing. He doesn't know anything. Incidentally, your last name is Allen. A-l-l-e-n."

Alan's lips twitched. "That should be easy to remember."

"So what did happen upstairs?"

"Nothing. Don't fuss."

They rejoined Selena and Serena at a long buffet table loaded with a mouth-watering assortment of hors d'oeuvres: smoked oysters, quail eggs, *foie gras*, artichoke leaves; Pauley had spared no expense.

"Super party," Selena said enthusiastically, popping a crab puff in her mouth. She caught Alan's eye. "Starving artist," she said thickly.

Serena nudged Hilary. "You make a good couple." She nodded at Alan. "You look right together."

"Thanks," Hilary said, surprised. Serena was the only friend that evening who had seemed to approve of Hilary's 'relationship.'

"Let me know when the time comes. I'd like to design your wedding rings."

"Wedding rings!" Hilary hastily lowered her voice. "Thanks for the offer but it's a little premature."

Serena studied Hilary with peculiar intensity in her tilted eyes. "There's something special between you. Some bond. I can feel it."

Sure, Hilary thought ruefully. Partners in crime. She watched Alan absently glance at his wrist, checking the time on a nonexistent watch. It was the third time that day Hilary had noted that automatic gesture.

Somewhere along the line Alan had lost his watch. Was that significant? She tuned back in to hear Serena conclude, "You can always tell the people who belong together." Her eyes wandered to the front entrance.

Hilary tried to think who hadn't arrived. She could think of no one Serena would be particularly interested in. Selena was right, something was definitely bothering her twin. Never had Hilary known Serena to be so quiet and preoccupied.

She watched the other woman's nervous start as Bryan Kinsale loomed up behind her, growling in champagne-soaked tones, "Hey, lovely lady, looking for me?"

Serena closed her eyes as though in pain. Selena remarked, "Now there's a rhetorical question if I ever heard one."

With the paranoia of the very drunk Bryan glared at the ring of watchful faces. His eyes fell on Alan. He focused with difficulty.

"Your name's Alan, isn't it?"

"Yes."

"You're English, huh?"

"British," Selena and Hilary chorused.

"Whatever," said Bryan. He continued to eye Alan. "Mate of mine's named Alan. He's English too. Maybe you know him?"

"Maybe."

"We were at art school together."

"Which art school was that?" Alan inquired.

Bryan opened his mouth, then a sly look came over his face. He shook his head. "Oh no, oh no. I'm not falling for *that*. It doesn't matter where I went to school. *She* never went to a damned art school." He pointed to Hilary. "Did you?"

"No."

"No," agreed Bryan. "Child prodigy stuff. She was doing Bible story coloring books when Pauley *discovered* her. That pompous ass Pauley! You know the biggest moment of his life? When he had his picture taken with effing Picasso. Why does the direction of art always rest in the hands of a few critics and dealers?"

"Why ask why?" drawled Selena.

"I'll tell you why," Bryan spat. "Money."

"Hey, it's what makes the world go round."

"*You* would think so."

"Yes, I would," Selena said. "I'm past the age where I think it's okay to mooch off friends. How many months overdue is your rent, Bry?"

Bryan wheeled, seeking whoever had betrayed this confidence. When he swung back to Selena, his brown eyes were more watery than usual. "What the hell do you know about art, Selena?" he quivered. "You sell T-shirts for a living."

"But I went to Art School," Selena mocked. "And not the one on the matchbook covers."

For a minute Bryan looked like was going to burst into tears. Instead he turned on heel, narrowly missing crashing into the buffet table before stumbling away.

Alan's eyes found Hilary's. She seemed unmoved by the scene they had witnessed. Perhaps it was a common occurrence?

Further discussion was hindered by Grainger clapping his hands from across the room.

"Attention everyone! May I have everyone's attention? Hilary, my pet, would you do the honors?" Grainger gestured towards the monolithic white cake.

Hilary muttered something under her breath and went to join Grainger in the center of the red carpeted floor. Accepting the knife he theatrically proffered she pretended to consider running him through.

There was laughter. Alan suspected more than a grain of genuine feeling behind the smattering of applause.

With all eyes focused on Hilary he had leisure to scan the crowd around him. There was no sign of Bryan Kinsale, which was a pity. If there was a weak link in this chain it was Kinsale. Alan spotted Selena and Serena whispering together, faces veiled behind the rippling curtain of their hair. On the crowd's fringe he glimpsed Rebecca Nash beside a tortured-looking piece of sculpture. Unobtrusively he edged to her side.

Becca greeted him with a preoccupied smile.

"Have I seen your paintings yet?"

"I'm afraid as a painter I was never much more than a good copyist." Becca nodded at the monstrosity of white stone looming over them. "This is mine."

Alan stepped back to examine the sculpture. Any comment

was forestalled by Grainger who launched into a long speech os-
tensibly in praise of Hilary but evolving into a sales pitch for the
gallery.

Grainger Pauley, Alan deduced, was a self-made man. Most of
the rough edges had been smoothed away with the same rigorous
discipline that kept Pauley's sixty-year old body in such excellent
shape. But all the polishing in the world couldn't conceal an ego
the size of Becca's sculpture. Not that ego was solely a criminal
trait.

Was his prejudice against Pauley influencing his judgment?
Alan thought not. He didn't like the man but he believed he was
able to view Pauley from an objective distance. Alan suspected he
was able to view most things from an objective distance. He sensed
this ability to detach himself was fundamental to his nature.

Now as to how he recognized a chic little number when he
looked at a dress, was something else again. He felt within himself
a certain level of experience with the female of the species. Enough
so that he could put a price tag on a dress, if not the actual girl. He
was quite sure that he never let physical desire cloud his reasoning.
He felt a wary, if tolerant view of women—perhaps he was comfortable with a level of sophistication, possibly even shallowness.
This might be one reason why Hilary made him uneasy. He didn't
understand her. He did understand that on no account must he
get personally involved with her. He could list a number of excellent reasons why; the fact that he felt he had to do so was what
alarmed him.

***

"My God, Grainger loves the sound of his own voice," Selena
groaned during the short drive home. "Poor Hil."

"He has his moments." Smothering a yawn, Hilary leaned back
into the solidity of Alan's shoulder. She considered whether to move.
It was extraordinarily comfortable. She decided to stay put. Alan
shifted to accommodate her.

Behind the steering wheel, Serena suddenly laughed for the first time that evening. "That cake!" she said. "Didn't it look like one of Becca's sculptures?"

The twins giggled merrily. Hilary glanced up at Alan in the darkness. He was faintly smiling. Something about that smile made her uneasy. It reminded her of the thin smiles on the faces of sitters in Renaissance portraits. Enigmatic, that was the word.

"The Campbells weren't there," Selena reflected aloud.

"Who are the Campbells?" Alan asked.

Selena shrugged a negligent shoulder. "The odd couple. He paints cowboy pictures. Charles Russell meets Leaning Tree calendars. That kind of thing."

"They're not cowboy pictures," Serena put in testily.

"*She,*" Selena went on, undisturbed, "is your standard issue surfer chick. She features prominently in Tom's paintings, usually as a golden-haired Indian maiden—stop me when you feel sick. Of course the most sickening thing about it is that Grainger handles Tom Campbell's work but won't handle Bryan's. And Bryan, whatever else he is, is a hell of a painter."

"Tom's work sells, which is why Grainger handles it."

Grainger's a snob," Selena argued.

Hilary became aware of how closely Alan followed this innocent exchange. Tonight he had listened and learned. Hilary wondered how ruthless Alan might be in using that knowledge.

***

It was in a pensive mood that Hilary bade the Thomases goodnight and walked up to the loft with Alan.

"Tea?" he inquired, closing the door behind them.

"No thanks." Hilary watched him at home in her kitchen, fixing tea. The incongruity of this masculine man performing such a domestic task brought a faint smile to her lips. Putting off the discussion she knew they must have, Hilary went to change.

When she returned to the front room Alan had donned the

Levi's and charcoal sweatshirt she had purchased for him that morning.

"Where are you going?"

"Back to Smuggler's Bay."

"*Why?*"

"To check out the house," Alan replied in tones of one pointing out the obvious.

It took Hilary a moment to believe what she was hearing. It took another moment before she could speak with any restraint. She wanted to howl her protest. "I didn't see the point of going back there this morning, and I sure don't see the point of going back there now! The sheriffs will have taken away whatever clues were there. In fact, they could still be watching the house."

"Most unlikely."

"What is this really about?"

"Investigation begins at the crime scene."

"What is that supposed to mean in real life?"

"Maybe once I'm inside the house I'll remember something. Perhaps I'll spot something the locals missed."

Maybe Alan was right. It was a cinch he knew more about this kind of thing than Hilary. But the risk seemed to far outweigh any possible gain.

She said urgently, "Listen, if you're caught in that house, it's all over. For both of us. You heard what Grainger said, the police are already asking questions about me."

Alan's head raised, green eyes gleaming. "I'm glad you brought that up, because there's no earthly way the police can have connected me to you this quickly. Not possibly. So what is your Mr. Pauley up to?"

"Why would Grainger lie?"

"No idea, but it's interesting don't you think?" When Hilary stood there without reply, he added, "Would you happen to have a pair of gloves?"

This snapped her out of her absorption. "Why do you need gloves? I thought your prints were all over the house."

"Fresh prints would indicate a return appearance, wouldn't they?"

Alan's snappishness indicated he was more on edge than he appeared. Hilary suspected he wasn't all that keen to go back to Smuggler's Bay either. Maybe the place held a morbid fascination for him. It was where his memories began.

"I can do gloves," she said finally. "What else do you need?"

Her capitulation seemed to drain the tension out of his taut frame. His tone was less abrupt as he tallied the things he needed.

When Hilary returned a few minutes later she had changed into black jeans and a black turtleneck.

"I'm going with you," she informed Alan handing over the items he had requested.

"No offense but I can move faster on my own."

"None taken. I am going nonetheless."

Without answering Alan stuck the flashlight in his back pocket. He slipped the gloves on testing for fit as he flexed his hand.

"Suppose you black out again?"

"I did not black out. I was dizzy for a moment."

"You might be developing complications from that blow on the head."

She was prepared to argue on but Alan sighed. "Very well. But you've got to agree to do exactly as I tell you."

"Naturally."

"And don't say I didn't warn you."

The first thing Alan had not warned Hilary about was that they were stealing a car. The Thomas's Renault, to be precise.

"Wouldn't it be easier to ask?" Hilary whispered when Alan's third attempt with the coat hanger through the window failed to unlock the door.

"It would undoubtedly be easier," Alan said from between his teeth, "but if our activities on this night ever come into question you may need an alibi."

This gave Hilary so much food for thought that she was still digesting once they were in the car. Alan fiddled with the steering wheel base and swore under his breath.

"Suppose Serena or Selena planned on using the car tonight?"

"Where would they be going at midnight?"

"Where are we going?"

Alan continued to rub wires together. There was a spark which made Hilary jump, and the engine rumbled into life. Alan straightened up, changed gears. He said, eyes in the rearview, "Selena was half-crocked. Serena is going to cry herself to sleep. Weren't you noticing?"

"I guess not." Hilary fell silent as they left the narrow streets of Steeple Hill sleeping in the moonlight, and Alan opened up the throttle.

***

The house stood tall and silent in the shadow of the pines. The yellow ribbon proclaiming POLICE LINE DO NOT CROSS moved gently in the breeze. There was no sign of life.

Hilary noticed a realtor's sign posted in the drying grass, which she had missed earlier that day. Alan slipped under the police tape; Hilary followed, her heart thudding, her hands sweaty in the latex gloves.

Their footsteps sounded unnervingly loud on the front walk.

Hilary waited, nearly dancing with nervousness while Alan applied the awl, which he had borrowed from her kitchen drawer, to the front door lock.

"Have you noticed how many criminal skills you possess?"

Alan finished jimmying the lock. Gently he pushed the door wide. The hinges shrieked in true haunted house fashion.

"It can't alarm you any more than it does me." He answered her and then stepped aside, mock-gallantly gesturing Hilary in.

"After you," she whispered.

The beam of his flashlight traveled across the bare floors and blank walls as Alan walked through the hall, past a staircase into a large room where bay windows looked out over the ocean. Over his shoulder Hilary could see the colored lights of Steeple Hill twinkling down the coast.

At the far end of the room was a stone fireplace. On the floor in front of the fireplace heart was the white chalk outline of a man.

The hair on the back of Hilary's neck rose as she stared at it. She watched Alan's silhouette move across the moonlit room. Impossible to know what was going through his mind as he too stared down at the chalked outline. A moment later he turned away, his flashlight beam probing into a corner of the room.

"I came to over there. By the door." His voice sounded emotionless, disembodied.

Hilary's gaze followed the path of light.

"He was kneeling beside me, going through my pockets. I think he'd just put my wallet in his pocket. That's my impression, but I was pretty groggy. He must have hit me when I came through the doorway. I think I groaned or tried to get up. He shoved me back, slammed my head against the floor. I lost consciousness for an instant. I remember bringing my arms up to break his hold. Somehow we both got to our feet. We tried to slam each other into the wall, anything to knock the other off his feet."

"Did you know who he was at that point?"

Alan shook his head slowly. "I suppose I must have. The only thing I know for sure is that if I'd gone down again I'd have been done for."

Hilary was silent.

"I used my weight to throw him off-balance. He went down and hit his head on the edge of the hearth. I think I passed out. When I came to the second time, he was dead and someone was banging on the front door. A cab driver, I think."

"A cabby? The papers never said anything about that."

Alan didn't seem to hear. "I knelt down by the body, felt his pockets. I found my wallet, stuffed it in my pocket and got out by that door." The flashlight beam swung over to the darkened doorway leading into the next room.

There was something here they were both missing, Hilary thought. Something obvious. Something to do with the cab driver.

"Alan," she exclaimed, "if a cab brought Napier, who brought you? And how could Napier have been in this house before you?"

Alan raised his hand cutting her off. His body tensed, listening.

Hilary heard it too: the crunch of footsteps on the gravel walk.

They both listened tautly and a moment later they heard the scrape of a key in the front door lock.

CHAPTER SIX

Hilary's brain had one horrified moment to register what was happening before Alan grabbed her, hustling her out the other doorway into a hall with a short flight of stairs at one end. The stairs led into another room. French doors opened onto a brick terrace.

Alan headed for the glass doors, prying at them with the awl.

Down the hall Hilary could hear the muffled approach of footsteps. She watched Alan struggle with the wired latch bolts. If he felt any of the panic coursing through her veins he didn't show it.

At last he jimmied free the second catch. He turned, finger to lips and beckoned to Hilary. Nodding understanding she tiptoed towards the adjoining room.

As she stepped forward one of the floorboards cracked loudly, unmistakably, the sound seeming to resonate through the empty house's dusty silence.

Hilary froze.

Alan moved fast, yanking open a side door and thrusting Hilary into a closet, taking the knapsack from her unresisting hands. His voice feathered against her ear. "Wait till it's all clear. Go out through the terrace. Climb down to the beach—"

"It's a sheer drop!"

"There's a path. I used it yesterday."

Yesterday? Was it only yesterday?

Her thoughts cut off abruptly as Alan kissed her, one hard, swift kiss. Before Hilary had time to react, he had closed the closet door, shutting her into a musty blackness. Unbelieving, Hilary stood motionless, blood roaring in her ears, wanting to scream denial and not daring to make a sound.

Footsteps pounded down the hall. Was Alan leading the in-
truder away? The floorboard groaned in the room where she hid.
Hilary shrank back into the stifling confines of her hiding place.

More footsteps; now running from the opposite direction.
These were followed by the report of a slamming door. How many
people were in this house? Something like a herd of elephants
crashed once more down the hallway.

Terrifyingly, a voice rang out, "Police. Stop or I'll fire!"

Hilary's heart stopped. Knuckles jammed to her mouth she
waited in agony to hear the sound of shots crashing throughout
the stillness.

There was nothing.

She could hear her wristwatch ticking. She could hear the blood
rushing in her ears. Then it came, a loud bang that caused Hilary
to cry out before she recognized the sound: a door slamming shut.

Then nothing.

Silence.

Darkness which may be felt.

It trickled into Hilary's mind that now was the moment she
was supposed to make her escape. *Move,* her brain commanded.
Go now. Her body remained paralyzed at the thought of abandoning
the relative safety of her hiding place.

Suppose the police . . .

But it was not the police. The police would have identified
themselves early on. The police would have fired warning shots.
The police would not have crept in on foot.

Who then?

The only thing Hilary knew for sure was that if she didn't
leave now the opportunity would be lost. Whoever was chasing
Alan would come back to the house and search for whatever Alan
had been looking for.

It took all Hilary's strength of will to reach unsteady fingers to
the closet door.

What if he's already returned? What if there's more than one of
them?

The door fell open on moonlight spilled over bare floorboards. The room was deserted.

Hilary crept forward. Ears straining she edged towards the doorway, flattening herself to the wall. She listened tensely. She peeked around the door frame.

Moonlight and shadows.

Ahead loomed the French windows and a view of the cliffs beyond. Hilary heard the front door close again. She heard footsteps approaching. Her heart leaped in her throat. She darted to the glass doors, easing them open, and slipped out into the windswept night.

She could smell the sea; hear its rumble below the cliffs.

Leaves crunched underfoot as Hilary ran lightly across the terrace, down the stairs and across the overgrown lawn. The wet grass soaked her sneakers. She trotted along the half-dead hedge, searching for the path Alan told her must be there. Blindly her hands rustled the branches seeking an opening in the hedge. A look over her shoulder at the house showed her the white circle of a flashlight beam stabbing against the darkened windows.

Every moment she expected to hear a shout behind her. And then, just as she began to lose hope, Hilary found the opening. Alan was right. A path from the yard led to stone steps built into the face of the cliff. The stairway vanished into inky blackness.

If Alan had managed these steps half-stunned then Hilary knew she could make it too. She was far more afraid of whoever was in that house. Still, she hesitated. The stairs were narrow. There was no rail or support on the seaward side. One slip and Hilary would be a footnote in an Art History textbook.

One hand braced on the cliff wall, she felt for the first step. Her foot scraped the sandy surface. She would have to take her time though every nerve in her body screamed for haste. Horror stories of falls and drownings came vividly to memory.

Two steps.

Three . . .

It seemed to Hilary that she had been feeling her way down

this cliff for hours. With every minute she expected to be discovered from above.

Fifteen.

Sixteen . . .

The further down the stairs she got, the colder it was. Hilary's nostrils quivered at the dank smell of the seawater swirling beneath her. The walls of the cliff became increasingly wet and slimy, the steps slick and treacherous.

To distract herself Hilary thought about Alan. He had to have escaped; his capture would have been far noisier, she reassured herself. So what would he do next? Where would he go? What should she do once she was out of here?

Step by step Hilary descended into what smelled and sounded like a watery dungeon. The noise level was deafening as the waves crashed against the rocks. Long before she reached the bottom Hilary realized that Alan had miscalculated one small point.

Yesterday, when Alan made his climb, the tide had been out, leaving an empty beach for him to hike to safety. Tonight the tide was in, and while it was not yet high, it was high enough to cover the last steps. In fact, as Hilary stepped off into the water with a loud splash she realized that the tide was nearly up to her thighs.

The waves were coming in fast, sucking the shifting sand out from under her feet. The cold water weighted her sodden clothes. She had very little time.

Steadying herself against the barnacled face of the cliff Hilary waded through water, alternately pushed and tugged back by the tide. *When I get to the beach I'll hike up to the highway,* she told herself. *I'll start walking back to town.* Hopefully Alan would spot her on the road.

On she went at a sloshing jog, not consciously admitting she was racing the tide, not consciously admitting her life was at stake. Once she fell to her knees and water closed over her head. Salt water filled her mouth, stung her eyes. Hilary hauled herself back on her feet, choking and gasping as she clung to the out-jutting rocks.

The Lord is my rock, and my fortress, and my deliverer, she prayed silently, hardly able to hear her thoughts over the roar of the ocean.

She ploughed on.

At last the cliffs gave way to boulders, then rocks, and finally Hilary found herself on an open stretch of sand. Parked on the crest of the hill, shining in the moonlight was the Renault. Alan was striding up and down the shoreline.

Lungs burning, legs leaden, Hilary staggered towards him. Spotting her, Alan ran forward.

"Where have you been? What happened to you?" Hilary could just make out these words over the crash of the waves. "I went back to look for you . . ."

She gasped out, "The tide came in," and sank into his arms. She felt Alan go rigid with shock, and raising her head decided the stricken expression on his face was some consolation.

Setting Hilary back on her feet, he helped her struggle out of her stiff clothing. She dragged the dripping turtleneck up over her head, tossing it to the sand as Alan reached for the button-fly of her jeans. There was nothing like the threat of freezing to death to banish little things like modesty or poor body image.

"H-hey, hey!" Hilary got out between chattering teeth as he knelt to yank her Levi's down. Hilary braced her hand on his shoulder, stepping out of the denims. She felt like she was moving in slow motion, shaking so with cold and fatigue that she could hardly balance.

Alan drew his sweatshirt over his head and settled the warm fleecy folds around Hilary's shoulders.

"T-thanks. I c-can do the rest."

"Turn around."

Alan unsnapped the hooks on her bra with the familiarity of one who's had plenty of practice removing women's intimate apparel. This scrap of cotton too joined the pile of clothes in the sand.

Hilary yanked the sweatshirt down over her breasts. It's warm folds grazed her thighs.

"Your knickers."

"My k-knickers are fine where they are. L-look, this isn't your fault."

Alan's eyes flew to Hilary's. He said nothing.

"Did you hear me?"

"I heard."

"Then—?"

"Stow it. You nearly drowned."

"I know. I was there. It was my choice to come. My decision."

"I shouldn't have let you make it."

"You couldn't have stopped me, short of knocking me out and tying me up. You can't take responsibility for something you had no control over."

"I have complete control."

Oh boy.

"What you have are delusions of grandeur. Or maybe a God complex. M-minor deity variety."

Alan ignored this, hustling Hilary up the hill to the car. Dumping her wet garments in the back, he walked around to the driver's side, sliding in beside her. He started the engine and switched the heater on full blast.

"How did you get away?" Hilary asked finally when halfway back to Steeple Hill Alan still showed no sign of breaking his taciturn silence.

"I used the awl to flatten his tire. He was parked on the road a few kilometers below us. It was sheer luck he didn't come around the bend and spot our car."

Hilary digested this. Clearly tonight had been hard on Alan's male ego in more way than one. *Complete control?* Being a perfectionist he focused on what had gone wrong rather than the fact that they had escaped alive.

She prodded finally, "You must have seen who it was?"

"Our friend, Scotland Yard."

"What was he doing there this time of night?"

Alan shrugged his bare shoulders. "Trying to catch who done

in his chief, I suppose." He sounded sardonic. "Ignoring procedure, bypassing chain of command, doing everything that got his Super killed."

"What got his Super killed," Hilary pointed out, "was trying to kill *you*. That's a little more serious than not filling out a Req. form in triplicate."

No comment.

Nothing more was said before they reached Steeple Hill. Alan parked the Renault exactly where they had found it on the shady, quiet street. He handed Hilary her wet clothes and bag, and sent her on ahead. Chilled to the bone, half-dead with exhaustion, Hilary had no energy for questions. She let herself into the dark building, still stuffy with the heat from the day, and sneaked up the stairs.

Safely inside the loft Hilary turned on the tea kettle and headed straight for the shower.

Alan had still not returned by the time she toweled down. Hilary changed into her sleep shirt and was sitting on the floor cradling a cup of chamomile tea, trying not to nod off when a hand on her shoulder had her starting up, sloshing tea over the cup rim.

"Sorry. Didn't mean to startle you." Alan's voice was weary.

Hilary blinked up at him. "I must have dozed off for a minute." Gingerly she straightened the crick in her neck. "I didn't hear you come in. What's the time?" She smothered a jaw-cracking yawn.

"Half-three." Alan's eyes seemed dark and unfathomable as he stared down at her.

In the muted light his skin had a warm, golden cast. Hilary's eyes swept up the tall lean length of him. Like Da Vinci's Universal Man, there wasn't an ounce of superfluous flesh on Alan. He was a study in perfect composition: broad shoulders, tapered hips, long legs. She couldn't ever remember feeling so attracted to a man, and her fingers clenched on the handle of the china cup.

Very carefully she set it aside. "What took you so long?" she asked to dispel the mood.

Alan's answer was prosaic enough. "I was changing the odometer back. It was more difficult than I anticipated. The car's an early model or I should never have managed it."

"But why bother?"

"Serena mentioned they'd had it serviced the day before yesterday. I want every mile on it accounted for on the off chance."

The off chance that they had cops banging on the door before breakfast.

"You are thorough."

"Am I?"

They were making conversation, keeping that vibrating aware-ness at bay. No sooner did Hilary recognize this then all her words dried up. It disconcerted her to realize how much she wanted Alan to wrap her up in his strong arms and comfort her in that most basic way.

Alan squatted, his eyes level with Hilary's. "About earlier . . . Nothing like that can happen again. You must see that. You must realize that this is not a game."

"I never thought it was a game."

"I don't know that I can protect you. I don't know that I can protect myself. I can't take that responsibility."

"I'm not asking you to take responsibility for me, Alan. I don't want that."

"One man is dead."

"And one man's life is at stake. Yours."

"Tonight your life was at stake. You nearly drowned. "

"I'm not afraid to take chances."

Hilary watched the Adam's apple move in Alan's throat. "I can't let you take that chance."

"You can't stop me."

She could feel him trying to whip up his anger. Could feel his weariness like her own, undermining his efforts.

"Don't make this harder than it is."

"I'm going to make it as hard as I can," Hilary said honestly. "We're in this together."

After a taut moment Alan hauled her into his arms. It was a

rough embrace, comforting rather than erotic. It took Hilary by surprise and she smoothed her hands over the hard planes of his back offering solace in return.

They stayed like that, motionless, for long minutes. With her head buried against Alan's bare shoulder Hilary breathed in the clean, male scent of him. She could hear his heart thudding steadily beneath her ear, hear each long, slow breath he took. She felt the warmth of his breath against her ear, stirring her hair.

"Alan?" she breathed.

"Hmm?"

"We have to slow down."

Alan's hands stilled on her shoulders. Hilary could feel tension running through him like a live wire. He said in a clipped tone, "You don't have to tell me. I've no intention of sleeping with you."

For the second time that night Hilary felt that she had been dumped into ice water. She pulled out of his embrace. "Your body is sending a different message. Anatomy's my thing, remember?"

Alan's mouth curved into a reluctant smile. "Fair enough. I do find you attractive."

"Don't tell me: it's nothing personal."

"Hilary, there's nothing on earth I'd rather than do than spend what's left of this night making love with you. It would mean every kind of pleasure and comfort to me. But I don't want to use you. I'm afraid that's what I would be doing."

"This isn't helping," Hilary told him exasperatedly.

Alan's hands tightened on her shoulders. "Then you're not listening to me. I care about you, Hilary. In little over twenty-four hours I've come to care very much."

"Life and death situations create a kind of instant intimacy," agreed Hilary. "How much of what we're feeling is genuine?"

Genuine sex maybe. Probably.

Alan said, "Correct. How can I trust my feelings when I don't remember anything before yesterday?"

Hilary sighed and once more leaned her head into Alan's chest, taking comfort from his warmth and nearness. How simple it would be if she was a different kind of person. If Alan was.

She knew that one concern Alan was not sharing was that he might be married. If his watch was missing, why not his wedding ring? At the very least he might be 'involved.' In fact it was pretty likely that a man as eligible as Alan *would* be involved with someone.

Hilary said at last, "At least we understand each other."

"Yes. Christ, it's hard having principles sometimes." There was such rueful candor in that they both laughed. Alan said, "At the risk of sounding like a bad movie or getting my face slapped, we've both had one *hell* of an evening. Could we just hold each other, do you think?"

"At the risk of getting myself into trouble, yes. I need someone to hold me tonight."

By way of answer Alan scooped Hilary up, rising easily to his feet and striding with her to the bed. He settled her between the soft white blankets and stretched down beside her.

Hilary's lashes lifted. "Any means of avoiding the futon, right?"

"Right you are."

Quite gently, as though she were very precious, very fragile, Alan gathered Hilary into his arms. She made a small sound of contentment and put her arms around him. Alan sighed, his breath whispering against her hair. Exhausted, Hilary closed her eyes and let herself fall into sleep.

***

She was a tall girl but she might have been custom-tailored to his body the way her curves fit sweetly into his hard angles. Two days ago he hadn't know she existed. Hard to believe, considering how familiar she seemed to him now. Not that it changed anything. They could stitch him up for this one, and the less involved he was with Hilary Jackson, the better for her. He had made the right decision.

Alan sighed. He felt her acutely all down the length of his

body; delicious torture. He could feel her muscles gradually relaxing as he caressed the nape of her neck beneath the silky, still damp hair. His own muscles felt rigid with the control he was exerting. Her breathing was soft and easy, whereas he had to regulate that as well.

Cautiously he shifted a little so as not to embarrass either of them with the increasingly obvious state of his arousal. He deserved sainthood for this. Well, she was the girl to appreciate that.

***

Hilary woke to the smell of fresh coffee and bacon frying, two of the best smells in the world. She could hear someone rattling around her kitchen. Comfortable, domestic sounds. She stretched, smiling sleepily and opened her eyes.

Rain drizzled against the tall windows. The world outside was a silvery blur of wet daylight. On the bright side, there were no cops breaking down the door. Hilary picked her wristwatch off the bed stand and peered at the time. Nearly nine. Half a day's light gone. She sat up, ruffling her hair briskly.

"Rise and shine."

Over her legs Alan set a wooden breakfast tray laden with bacon, scrambled eggs and croissants still hot from the bakery near the park.

"Wow. I'm impressed."

She meant the food but she could just as easily have been referring to Alan. This morning he wore his faded Levi's and nothing else. The Levi's fit low on his hips, emphasizing his flat stomach and long legs. Even his feet were well-shaped, Hilary reflected wryly, as Alan sat down on the foot of the mattress. She scooted her legs over, making room.

"You've had a busy morning."

"The game's afoot, Watson." He tossed the newspaper folded neatly on the tray to Hilary who smoothed out the front page.

POLICE BAFFLED proclaimed the headline. This was news?

"Something interesting there," Alan remarked, following the progress of Hilary's eyes down the printed page.

"Because this is just a re-hash of yesterday's article?"

"Not exactly. It appears the sheriff's keeping a lid on this."

"What makes you think so? Maybe they don't have any new information." She watched Alan select a strip of bacon from her plate. A bacon and eggs kind of guy then.

"Check out the editorial on page three. Topic? Restraint of the free press."

Hilary whistled. "What do you think it means?"

"The police may have information they don't want released to the general public." Alan shrugged. "Or sometimes it means they have a direct lead and they don't want the suspect getting wind of it."

Hilary stared at the photo midway down the front page.

"That's Napier?"

"Yes."

She studied the picture. It was a lousy photograph, no doubt taken from a passport. She wasn't sure what she had expected but it wasn't that Napier would look like Serpico. The man from Scotland Yard had had longish dark hair and sported a beard. His eyes had photographed in that colorless fashion pale blue eyes often do.

"Did you ever see him before?" Alan asked, watching her face.

"No. I don't think so."

"You don't sound sure."

"There's something familiar about him. How old was he?"

"Something younger than myself." Alan's voice sounded remote. "Why?"

Why indeed? Did it make a difference that Napier wasn't middle-aged and paunchy? That he didn't fit her image of a bad cop, of a burn-out, of a cop on the take?

"Just curious. There's a whole article on him."

"That I can do without."

Alan seemed to display near-aversion for anything to do with Napier.

"I think the key to this whole thing revolves around Napier." Absently she picked up a slice of bacon, nibbling it. "I think understanding his character is intrinsic. After all, if he was a bad cop—"

"They'll have my prints from the house," Alan interrupted, his thoughts running at a tangent. "The Yard will have provided a match by now."

"Maybe you don't have a record."

"Maybe."

"Why are you so sure you're a crook?" Hilary examined the shoulder Alan presented to her. His damp hair curled black against the nape of his neck. She found something fascinating in the contradiction of baby-smooth skin and taut muscle, in the contrast of light and dark texture. Once again she was struck by the desire to sketch him.

"Let's see. Last night alone I hot-wired and stole a car. I picked a lock and broke into a house. I resisted arrest. I flattened a police vehicle tire."

"You exceeded the speed limit," Hilary put in helpfully.

"I killed a cop," Alan said harshly.

"No, that was the day before."

Alan stared at her speechlessly.

Hilary met that look compassionately. "Alan, why are you so ready to believe the worst of yourself? It seems to me that if these things you've done bother you so much, you can't be a very hardened criminal."

"Then explain—"

"I can't," Hilary admitted. "But I know there has to be some explanation. You don't *seem* like a criminal, Alan."

Alan said dryly, "It's a misconception of the general public that criminals 'seem' any different from themselves." He moodily ate the rest of his bacon.

"Okay, for example, that remark," Hilary observed. "I don't think criminals talk that way."

"How many criminals do you know, Hilary?"

"According to you, more than I realize."

No answering smile.

"However you figure it, this doesn't add up to a simple case of homicide. Or even accidental homicide." Hilary tapped the newspaper. "This reminds me. Napier arrived by taxi. The paper says that the taxi driver discovered his body."

"So?"

"So how did you get to the house?"

"What?"

"How did you get to Smuggler's Bay?" Hilary repeated patiently. "It's too far to walk from either direction. The police never found an abandoned car. The taxi driver claims he didn't see another car. So how did you get there?"

"The bus?"

"The bus comes once in the morning and once in the afternoon."

Alan stopped chewing.

"Who drove you to meet Napier? What happened to this person after you escaped by the cliffs? If you also came by taxi, or if someone dropped you off, why didn't Napier's taxi driver, who was parked right out in front, see you arrive?"

"I must have arrived first. But no," Alan denied quickly. "I couldn't have. Napier—"

"Napier was already inside the house." Hilary finished his thought. "Last night you said Napier jumped you. That means he had to be in the house first. He had to be lying in wait for you."

"There's a flaw in your logic," Alan objected. "The fact that Napier knocked me cold doesn't mean I didn't try to jump him first."

"Alan, come on! Granted I've never seen you in . . . um . . . action, but I refuse to believe that if you were ambushing someone you'd blow it so badly that *you* were knocked out!"

That drew a reluctant smile from Alan.

"So see," Hilary concluded cheerfully, "You may be an outlaw, but Napier wasn't necessarily one of the good guys. I think it's possible he was a bad cop. Maybe he was up to something and maybe you might have had the . . . the.."

"Goods on him?" Alan supplied gravely.

"Laugh if you want, but it makes as much sense as anything you've come up with."

"I'm not laughing," Alan told her. He sat for a few moments staring out the window while Hilary sipped her ginseng tea. "What about the money?" he questioned finally.

"I don't know." Hilary shrugged. "Probably the only person with the answer to that question is whoever drove you to Smuggler's Bay. But I don't think we should assume the money was a payoff for killing Napier. There could be any number of excuses for that cash."

Alan couldn't think of another one that made any sense, but he didn't like to point this out to Hilary. Nor did he tell her that to whoever had paid him that blood money he must be looking more and more like a liability—and with him, Ms Hilary Jackson. The biggest favor he could do her was to get as far away from her as possible.

Hilary set down her empty cup. "Steeple Hill's art community is a small one. After last night I have a feeling that whoever is behind this—whatever this is—must know that we are . . . um . . . together."

Alan turned to her. "You think if I were to bail they might come after you?"

"It's possible, don't you think?"

Yes, he did think.

Not that he had planned to go far; just far enough to make it look like they'd parted company. He recognized that her accurate reading of him left him uncomfortable, as did her dispassionate assessment of her own situation. This was not feminine behavior he was familiar with.

"If you feel there is risk to you, of course I won't leave," Alan said.

"I feel there's risk to both of us."

***

Their next move was the Seven Palms Hotel in San Francisco. The Seven Palms was one of the last bastions of an all but vanished era of gentility and elegance. There were fresh flowers in all the rooms, monogrammed linens, and uniformed bellboys. High tea was served daily.

"Better than I hoped for," Alan said, returning to the Renault where Hilary waited behind a copy of the *Steeple Hill Gazette* Sunday edition. "They still use a registry book to back up the computer."

"How do you plan to get a look at it?"

"Book a room naturally."

Hilary tore her gaze from the long pool of fountains lined with the seven famous palm trees, plumy fronds waving against the steel plate skies. "Right. You're going to book a room. With cash. That's not suspicious. What am I going to do?"

"Create a diversion."

"Swell. Something I'm really good at: throwing scenes in public." She eyed Alan with misgiving. "Why don't I book the room and *you* throw the scene? I have a feeling you'd be so much better at it."

"I don't want to draw any attention to myself if I can help it."

Hilary sighed. "Okay-dokey. I'll throw a scene. Any suggestions? I don't have to scream fire or pretend to be epileptic, do I?"

"Definitely not. What about lost reservations? In fact, I just saw a couple checking into the bridal suite."

Hilary grimaced, staring down at her Levi's and T-shirt which proclaimed, *The Arts Are Not a Luxury.* "Sure, don't I look like a bride?" She nudged her tapestry bag with her foot. "I presume my trousseau is in here?"

Alan grinned.

***

Nearly twenty minutes later Hilary climbed back into the

Renault to find Alan, seat comfortably tilted back, doing the *Steeple Hill Gazette's* Sunday Crossword.

"I hope it was worth it," she told him, slamming shut the car door with extra vigor. "I've just spent the most humiliating fifteen minutes of my life."

Alan folded the paper up. "You were brilliant. I could have photocopied the ruddy book and they wouldn't have noticed. I'd no idea you had that kind of range."

"Dramatic or vocal?"

"Either. Both. Your better half had all our sympathies."

Hilary said without rancor, "I could learn to hate you."

Alan glanced up and laughed.

"When did you slink off?"

"Just as you were realizing you had the wrong hotel."

Hilary moaned, putting her hands over her face, remembering. "Tell me it was not in vain. Were you booked in here?"

"I checked for names with the starting initials A.X. No go. I tried X.A. Finally I just looked for anyone named Alan, first or last name. Still no good."

"You don't look particularly disappointed."

Alan's eyes gleamed like polished jade. He was smiling that peculiar little half smile.

"So what did you discover?"

"Something equally promising. Sir Alexander Napier has a room here."

CHAPTER SEVEN

"What if this is a trap?" Hilary whispered.

Alan's brows drew together but he didn't look away from picking the old-fashioned lock of Napier's hotel room.

"Wouldn't his sergeant know where he was staying?"

"My gut tells me Napier was flying solo on this one." Alan withdrew his makeshift lock-pick with a grunt of satisfaction.

From down the hall came the rattle of crockery and the squeak of wheels. Alan took Hilary into his arms, turning her against the enameled surface of the door, his body shielding hers from possible recognition.

From behind Hilary was sure it looked like an intimate little scene. From where she stood, every nerve-ending vibrating with consciousness of Alan's body, it felt transparently staged. Her eyes searched Alan's. Beneath dark lashes his eyes met hers unsmilingly.

A moment later he reached up and casually tucked a strand of hair behind her hair. Hilary blinked. Maybe he had a neatness fetish?

The bus boy pushed his cart up the hall. Three doors past where they stood, he hammered on the door.

"Room service!"

Hilary's eyes fell from the mouth a kiss away from her own. Last night Alan had kissed her a few seconds before he shut her into the closet, but that kiss had been as hard and brief as a salute before going into battle. She couldn't help but wonder what it would be like to be really kissed by Alan.

To shut out temptation Hilary closed her eyes. A little shock went through her as Alan's mouth touched hers in a whisper of a kiss that was almost a question.

She smiled against Alan's lips. There was an infinitesimal hesitation. Then his mouth moved against hers with unexpected hunger. The urgency of that kiss took Hilary aback, but it delighted her too. After a startled moment she responded whole-heartedly, locking her arms around his neck. Alan's breathing changed, his hands bit into Hilary melding her closer.

The bus boy rolled past, cart creaking.

Hilary couldn't help it. She laughed. Alan grinned, gazing down into Hilary's eyes. He raised his hand and lightly stroked her cheek and Hilary shivered involuntarily. With a wry smile Alan reached past her, turned the brass knob and pushed open the door to Napier's hotel room.

To Hilary's intense relief no one waited inside the room.

Of course not. She had not really expected to walk into a trap, and yet . . .

She closed the door behind them and turned to survey the old-fashioned room curiously, the dark paneling, antique furniture, and red velvet draperies. An oil painting of a Venetian palazzo hung over the bed. Hilary recognized the Holiday Inn School of Art.

It gave her a queer feeling to see Napier's personal belongings neatly laid out, waiting for the man who would never return to claim them. She wandered over to the bureau. A leather kit bag embossed in gold A.J.N. was surrounded by scattered articles: a silver-backed brush, a silver comb and a silver shaving mug all monogrammed A.J.N.

"Was the man having an identity crisis or what?"

"Hmm?"

Hilary glanced at Alan. From behind the bed headboard he had fished out a leather portfolio. He rapidly scanned its contents.

"What are we looking for?"

"Anything. Everything."

"I suspect everyone and no one," quoted Hilary.

"What's that?"

"That narrows it down." Hilary reached for the kit bag and Alan's head jerked up.

"Gloves."

"Sorry. Right." Hilary pulled out a pair of the latex gloves she bought by the box for working, and slipped them on. Gently she sifted through Napier's bag.

"I'm surprised he doesn't have a silver toothbrush. Did himself proud, did our Sir Alex. You don't earn money for these kinds of trinkets on a cop's salary, unless you Brits pay your police a lot better than we do."

No comment from Alan.

"Find anything?" Hilary inquired.

Again Alan didn't seem to hear, absorbed in his reading. Hilary raised her brows then went back to her own search.

She discovered little except that Sir Alexander, like Oscar Wilde, was only satisfied with the best. Sterling toilet articles, custom-tailored shirts, a green silk dressing gown.

"He wasn't planning on staying long," Hilary remarked to Alan's silent figure.

"No, his return ticket is here."

Stranger in a strange land.

Hilary began to feel depressed. Until now Alex Napier had been nothing more than a name and a blurry photo; but standing in this room, handling his private belongings she was touched by the knowledge that a real man had lived and died—died violently. A man who had preferred boxer shorts and an old-fashioned razor. She even found poignancy in a pair of tortoise-shell reading glasses on the bed stand.

Hilary opened the closet door. An olive green mac hung inside. She caught a whiff of masculine fragrance, something clean and spicy. Quickly she shut the closet door.

The fact remained that Napier had done his best to slay Alan in cold blood. Napier had lain in wait and he had tried to kill and then rob Alan. Whatever Alan was involved in, whether art theft or forgery, Napier had also been part of. The man had been a crook.

Hilary was certain of it, and although it was sad that he was dead, sad for his wife and children if he had any, it would have been much sadder if Alan had died in Napier's place.

She glanced at Alan, something in his silence catching her attention. He was sitting on the bed holding some newspaper clippings. She watched him massaging his forehead with the heel of his hand.

"What's wrong?"

"Nothing. Headache." Alan sounded uncharacteristically irritable.

Hilary came over to the bed and sat down beside him.

"What did you find?"

Alan opened his eyes, instinctively resisting Hilary's move to take the clippings. Then he seemed to give it up, sitting motionless as Hilary read down the *London Times* column, frowning.

LORD HENRY ARCHIBALD SLAIN

All England was shocked and saddened yesterday by the death of one of her national figures, Lord Henry Archibald, MBE, former commissioner of Scotland Yard and a hero of World War II. The tragedy occurred late Tuesday evening when Lord Henry surprised a burglar at his Surrey estate. After brutally striking down the 93 year old statesman, Lord Henry's assailant fled taking with him Rembrandt's famous Biblical painting of *Ruth* valued at over L1.2 million . . .

The article related Lord Henry's fifteen year stint as Commissioner of Scotland Yard and then detailed his impressive war record.

Cursorily Hilary glanced at the underlying clippings. Most pertained to Lord Henry's murder and the missing Rembrandt, but one story had to do with a second robbery, involving the theft of a Turner. Still another article had to do with the discovery of a stolen Renoir in the estate of a recently deceased art collector. There was yet another piece on a Japanese collector's discovery that his Manet was a forgery.

What was the link, Hilary wondered? There had to be one. Where did Napier and Alan fit into all this?

"Do you remember something about this?" she probed, turning to Alan. "Did you know this Lord Henry maybe? Napier seems
to link his murder with these other thefts."

Alan pinched the bridge of his nose, his eyes shut.

"Brilliant deduction."

Alerted by the sarcasm in Alan's tone, Hilary's eyes flicked over
his stony features. Had he lost color since they entered Napier's
hotel room? His eyes meeting hers looked almost black.

"Alan, what's the matter?"

The line of Alan's jaw was so tense Hilary's ached in sympathy.
He nodded toward the remaining cuttings she held.

"Keep reading."

Doubtfully Hilary turned back to the neatly clipped press re-
lease. The piece was a promo on the Pauley Galleries. Following
this were two articles on Hilary Jackson and a review of her show
last year at the Guggenheim Museum in Soho.

Hilary studied the clippings without comment.

Alan observed her dark brows arch and then draw together.

When she finished reading she handed Alan back the clippings.
"Napier believed that I was involved in these thefts?"

"A logical deduction."

He took perverse pleasure in her confusion. Alan felt an
unfamiliar desire to lash out, to be the utter and complete bastard
he was capable of being, to take it all out on Hilary. Anything to
push aside the cold, sick panic he had felt from the minute he
waked into this room. Napier's room with Napier's things strewn
everywhere waiting for a man lying on a slab in the morgue.

But it was more than this room. It was Lord Henry Archibald's
face beaming genially out of the pages of newspaper cuttings. Lord
Henry who he had last seen in a flashback with his bald egg head
smashed in. This room with its dark wood and long red draperies
reminded him of red damask draperies in that other room. The
room where Lord Henry had lain in his blue smoking jacket and
slippers and blood.

Alan's head was thumping in time with the thud of his heart.

He could barely hear Hilary's cool, clear voice over the beating in his ears.

"Are you trying to tell me you believe I'm involved in this?"

"I don't think you actually nicked the stuff, no. I don't think you coshed Lord Henry or had anything to do with setting up Napier."

"You're losing it, Alan," Hilary informed him.

"Am I?"

"Yep."

Until now one of the things Alan had chiefly liked about Hilary was her even temper. She was the easiest girl to get along with. No moods, no games. But now he gazed into those blue eyes and saw them fierce and calm as one of the Old Testament gals. He recognized that here was a woman he could have a knock down, drag out fight with, and she would roll with the punches and give as good as she got. It was an oddly liberating sensation.

"Say what you will, Napier knew his stuff. He drew his conclusions from fact."

"What facts, Alan? I'm a painter. That's the only fact I know of. I live in Steeple Hill with a lot of other painters, and Napier for some reason zeroed in on Steeple Hill. Whatever his *conclusions,* Napier was wrong because I'm *not* involved. Or if I am, it's through meeting you."

"You're forgetting another obvious link," Alan pointed out, reaching for one of the clippings she still held. "The Manet was a forgery."

"Oh, I get it. You think I'm forging the world's masterpieces and selling them through the Pauley Galleries? Grainger will love this."

Alan gazed down at the papers in his hand. He didn't honestly believe Hilary was forging paintings. Given her stature as an artist it would be most unlikely. He couldn't believe she was knowingly involved at all. But if he could pick a fight with Hilary he didn't have to visualize Lord Henry's crunched head.

"By the way," Hilary added, "You're assuming that your theory was Napier's. Napier isn't actually here to propound his theory. And why isn't he here? Did *I* kill him?"

Blimey. Alan stared as Hilary continued to muse in that chilly tone unlike any he'd her use before, "The part I can't figure is what do I need a gang of art thieves for? I can buy a three dollar copy of the *Mona Lisa* any time."

Not the *Mona Lisa,* Alan thought with grim enlightenment. Nothing that big. No, more like choice pieces such as Rembrandt's *Ruth* stolen in highly publicized crimes and then sold to unscrupulous collectors.

But then why the need for a forger? *Was* he assuming too much? Napier could have been working a number of cases. They needn't be connected. Why should the thieves need a forged copy of the paintings they stole when they had the paintings themselves?

Alan's line of thought was interrupted by Hilary's voice.

"I need to know. Do you believe I am involved in this, whatever this is?"

Her eyes met his and Alan's heart quailed as he recognized the wintry shimmer in her eyes, the austere line of her mouth. How could he explain that when he couldn't trust himself, when all his suspicions, fears, even memories indicated *he* was in it up to his neck, his first reaction (born of a life of cynicism) was *not* to trust.

"Hilary . . ."

Hilary made a sharp movement. "Yes or no, Alan. Explanations make it worse."

"I . . . don't know."

"You have no instinct on this?"

"I suppose I do."

"Let's not waste any more time sitting here."

"Hilary—"

She rose. "Anything else here you want to scope out? Obviously Napier wasn't worried about his things being searched since he left his casebook conveniently here for us to find."

"Hilary—damn! Would you shut up for a moment and listen to me? I was *there.*" Alan waved the handful of clippings. "I *remem-*

ber being there, I remember seeing—" He swallowed hard on the rest of it.

Yet he could not believe it. Refused to believe he had anything to do with that old man's death. Napier, yes. He could believe he'd killed Napier—and not for the money. He hated Napier. He had felt that hatred in his dream. He had wanted to kill Napier then, to slowly choke the life out of him. But a 90 year-old man? Not accidentally, not in self-defense, and not for a bloody painting. No.

But then why had he been there? Why had he let it happen? If he'd permitted murder to happen he was just as guilty as the man who had wielded the poker.

Hilary said curtly, "Do you remember killing him?

"I'm not—it's not clear." His head pounded furiously. Alan put his hands up, heels to his eyes.

"What do you remember?"

Alan tried to push past the pain, to *see* it. He gasped aloud as his head seemed to split apart.

Sirens. Police lights like strobes, flashing blue and red in the night. Frost on the ground. In the air. Static voices on police radios. The crunch of police issue on gravel. And the unmistakable scent of death hitting him as he walked through the doorway.

Slowly, through the mists, he became aware that Hilary was standing, dialing the white and gold phone.

"What are you doing?" His voice came out thickly.

"There's a number scribbled across the face of this scenic guide. I didn't see it at first because the ink blends into the blue of the bay." She wasn't looking at him, edgily tapping a pencil on the tabletop.

They were both silent as the phone rang on the other end. It rang and rang, shrilling away in the emptiness.

After 20 rings Hilary hung up.

"This is a local area code. That means this number doesn't belong to anyone in Steeple Hill. Not to the Pauley Galleries, and not to me. It's not a hotel because the front desk would be answering. It's probably not any kind of a business or an answering machine would pick up."

"I don't follow."

"It must be a residence."

"It could be a business line. A phantom number."

"If Napier wrote this number down it's probably worth investigating." She was still not looking at him. Probably just as well. Alan was afraid his face would reveal too much.

Hilary pulled open the bed-stand drawer and hauled out a thick phone directory.

"Why don't we try the obvious for a change?" She ran her finger down the printed page.

Fine, Alan thought, but what was obvious?

"Here we go. Xanders, Xenon, Xenophone," mused Hilary to herself. "Xeres, Alan. Well well." She looked up meeting Alan's gaze with one of triumph. "A.X. Guess what?"

"What?"

"The phone number is a match."

Alan wiped his forehead with his arm. The room felt hot. Stifling.

"Is there an address?"

"You betcha. We can be there within the hour."

"Then let's do it."

***

It was nearly tea time by the time they reached the two story duplex Alan Xeres rented on a tidy residential street off Lombard. Loud TV blared from the apartment next door. Kids played softball undeterred by the rain puddles and the street's steep rise. Sooty skies lowered over silvery roof tops.

They climbed the stairs to Alan's apartment and Alan knocked briskly on the redwood door.

"Why are you knocking?"

"There may be a flat mate."

Alan's roommate. A possibly female roommate, come to think of it, reflected Hilary with a wedge in her throat.

They waited in silence.

A scrawny gray cat wandered out of the shrubbery in the garden below. It darted up the stairs towards them, and wound ingratiatingly around Hilary's ankles. She stooped to pet it.

"There's a double deadbolt on this door," Alan informed her, inspecting the lock critically. "We're not getting in through here."

"We're not scaling the walls in broad daylight, I hope?"

The cat went to the door and meowed loudly at Alan.

"No, we'll come back after dark." He looked down at the cat. "You must be related. You have the same eyes."

"Mm." The cat meowed at him again. Alan gestured for Hilary to precede him down the wooden stairs.

Back in the car Alan drummed his fingers on the dashboard, looking hard through the windshield at the trim suburban neighborhood. After a few minutes he burst out, "None of this feels familiar. I can't believe I could live here and not remember anything."

"But you don't remember anything, do you?"

"No, but . . ." He groped for the words to explain. "This place isn't somewhere I'd live. Neither the neighborhood or the house."

"Why? There's nothing wrong with the neighborhood or the house."

"But I wouldn't live here. I'd know if I lived here. There's nothing remotely familiar about any of this."

"As opposed to . . .?"

Alan lifted an irritable shoulder.

"Was there anything familiar about Napier's hotel room?" Hilary persisted.

"Not particularly."

"Well then?"

"But there was—I don't know how to explain it. When I was reading those clippings, it was a shock but at the same time in the back of my mind I knew that this was something I already—"

"Didn't want to remember?"

Alan grimaced.

"That makes sense," she agreed. "Especially if you believe you were involved in Lord Henry's murder. But this is where Alan Xeres lives. It's too big a coincidence that Napier would have the same phone number but it belongs to *another* A.X."

"Quite."

Alan stared grimly out the windshield. Hilary said hesitantly, "*Is* the name Alan Xeres familiar to you?"

"Yes."

"But is it your name?"

Alan raked a hand through his dark hair, expelling a long sigh. "I don't know."

Although she had posed the question Hilary was taken aback by Alan's answer. "Who else would you be?"

"I don't know."

"How many people can be involved in this?"

No reply.

Apparently Alan had assumed that the moment he was back on his own turf his memories would snap into place. Hilary didn't know anything about amnesia but she suspected that this would have been a little too convenient.

"Maybe once you're inside something will click." She tried to reassure, "Maybe you're not here often enough to notice the neighborhood much."

Alan shrugged again, unconvinced.

***

They ate a quick meal at a coffee shop a few blocks from where Alan Xeres lived. The coffee shop was crowded. They squeezed into two seats at the counter and ordered burgers and fries. The close presence of other diners and the harassed waitress made real conversation difficult. Hilary felt that it would be difficult in any case. There was a definite strain between them.

Picking at their food, they made the polite conversation of strangers, leaving as soon as it was dark, and driving back to Alan Xeres' duplex. By then the tenant in the bottom apartment was home, lights on and stereo blasting.

"Here's the plan," Alan instructed as they pulled up once more in front of the duplex. "I'm going to try and get in through the back. Wait ten minutes and go round the front. See what you can learn from the chap downstairs. Then tell him you're going up to leave a message on the door. If all goes well I'll be able to let you in."

"Won't the . . ."

But Alan was already out of the car, a long shadow moving across the lawn and disappearing into the darkness. Hilary closed her mouth with a snap. Perhaps it was a kind of compliment that Alan took it for granted she would carry out his orders without a lot of detailed direction.

She waited exactly ten minutes, ears straining through the beat of reggae music for any sound to indicate Alan had failed, been caught . . .

All Quiet On The Western Front.

Hilary got out of the car and walked slowly up the path to the front door. It took several knocks before the door opened. A tall young black man with dread-locks stood in the light.

"I'm looking for Alan," Hilary called over the music.

The young man peered at Hilary through the screen. He snorted. "You and everyone else. The police were here this morning."

"The police?" Hilary felt her smile freeze. "Do you know why?" She turned as the gray cat they had seen earlier minced out of the wet ivy. The cat wound familiarly about Hilary's ankles purring.

"Nope. Didn't ask. None of my business."

"Do you know how long Alan's been gone?"

"Beats me. He comes and goes. I've been on the road the last two weeks." The genial giant smiled, teeth very white. "I'm a musician."

"Really? Wow." Hilary glanced down at the cat. "Yours?"

"No way. Xeres'. I'm allergic to cats. Bad for the pipes. I wish the Pound would pick it up. Xeres' leaves the frigging thing for weeks at a time."

Clearly this was a long standing grievance. Hilary said hastily, "Yeah well, I'm going to run upstairs and leave a note on the door, if that's okay?"

"Okay by me."

The door closed once more. Out went the porch light. Hilary walked around to the side of the building and climbed the wooden stairs, the cat complaining at her heels. As she reached the landing, the door to Xeres' apartment opened soundlessly.

Alan held open the screen and Hilary walked into the dark flat. From downstairs came the muffled thump of reggae. Alan shut the door and switched on the light.

"The shades are drawn."

Hilary relaxed and looked about herself. Unlike any other bachelor pad she had been in, Alan's apartment was clean as a whistle, and nearly as impersonal as it was immaculate.

The furniture was classic doctor's waiting room: low slung leather sofa and chairs, glass and oak coffee table. There was a matching oak entertainment center with stereo, television and VCR. The rooms smelt of Pine Sol and emptiness.

"What do you think?" Hilary watched Alan prowl through the stereo cabinet.

"About what?"

"Anything ring a bell?"

"No."

The cat, which had slipped in when Alan opened the screen, stood in the dark kitchen, tail twitching. Now it wove its way around Alan's legs and mewled its demands.

"You don't know this cat? It knows you."

Alan raised a skeptical brow.

"Well, I'm going to feed it anyway," Hilary said. "The man downstairs says it's Xeres' cat. He also said the police were here this morning."

"I thought I recognized their delicate touch." Alan had completed his check of the record cabinet and was kneeling by the sofa feeling under the cushions.

Hilary pulled her gloves out and slipped them on. A brief search discovered a shelf stacked neatly with cat food tins. She opened a can, set the cake on a plate and left the cat to it.

She found Alan going through the bedroom. "Find anything interesting?"

"Not so far." Alan ran his hands beneath the mattress

Hilary opened the closet and inspected the sizable, if unimaginative, array of white and blue tailored shirts.

"Could a man this neat be all bad? He even hangs up his pajamas."

"I don't wear pajamas," Alan muttered, searching the other side of the bed. "I don't listen to Neil Diamond or Barbara Streisand, and I don't like the paintings on the wall."

"They are pretty awful." Hilary inspected a gloomy study of Fisherman's Wharf. The signature at the bottom was AX.

She crossed to the oak chest of drawers and pulled out the top drawer. "Do you wear briefs or boxers, Alan?"

"I'm wearing briefs, which you bought. I prefer boxers."

Pristine briefs lay in three neat stacks inside the drawer.

"How can you remember the type of underwear you prefer but not your name?" Hilary was a little irked at that 'which you bought' reproof.

Alan, on one knee beside the bed, pulled open the bed stand drawer. "I imagine it's fundamental, Hilary. You don't forget your personal tastes."

'Hilary.' She had to admit she liked the way he rolled her name off his tongue in that oh-so-veddy accent. It was hard to stay angry at a man you liked so much. Hilary reported, "No photos, no letters; his bills are all paid. He doesn't appear to read. Doesn't even take a magazine. It's hard to learn anything from someone this meticulous. Even his garbage is tidy."

Alan was thumbing through a small black leather book. He

sat down on the edge of the bed. "Quite a ladies man, our Alan," he remarked. "With a four star rating system."

"Anything under Jackson?"

"Hmmm. No."

"My secret is safe."

Alan's lips pursed in a soundless whistle. "Hello, what's this?"

"What's what?" Hilary wandered over to the bed and peered over his shoulder.

"Under 'K.' Bryan Kinsale. Isn't that—?"

"Yes." Hilary examined the number. "It looks right. It's the right area code and prefix."

"Now that is interesting."

"Bryan didn't seem to know you," Hilary said slowly. "Unless he was faking."

"Exactly. Which leaves one of two possibilities." Alan's eyes were green as winter grass. "Either Bryan was faking for reasons that should prove interesting, or—"

"Or you're not Alan Xeres," Hilary finished reluctantly.

CHAPTER EIGHT

"If you're not Alan Xeres, who are you?" Hilary asked reasonably. "Where is Alan Xeres?"

"I don't know."

"Wait." Hilary raised one hand traffic warden fashion. "I'm confused. You're trying to tell me that besides Napier and Alan Xeres there was a *third* person—yourself—at Smuggler's Bay?"

"I suppose so."

"Or were you actually the fourth person? You must have been unless Xeres drove you to Smuggler's Bay himself. You should have sold tickets, half the county seems to have been there."

Alan directed towards Hilary what in novels used to be called a 'speaking glance.'

"Which brings us to the sixty-four thousand dollar question of who *is* Alan Xeres and why are we so sure he is involved?"

"The police think he's involved or they wouldn't be searching his flat," pointed out Alan. "The note with the money was addressed to AX. He has Bryan Kinsale's name in his directory. And I remember his name. It's one of the few things I do remember."

The cat wandered in from the kitchen and affectionately butted its head against Alan's legs. Meeting Hilary's gaze, Alan laughed unwillingly.

"It's not my cat."

"But none of this makes sense," Hilary protested. "You said your name was Alan. You had the note addressed to AX. All these clothes are the right size and very similar to what you were wearing that day."

"When you eliminate the impossible, whatever remains, no matter how improbable . . ."

"And love means never having to say you're sorry. Be serious, Alan."

"How the hell do you suppose I feel?" Though Alan kept his voice low nervous tension crackled in the air like static electricity. "I'm the one without an identity. Do you think it's easy to carry on not knowing who I am? Where I belong? Whether I have a family waiting for me somewhere? Whether I've killed a man? I tell you I am as sure as I can be that I never lived here, and you look as though you think I'm cracking up. I'm beginning to wonder myself."

Abruptly, the stereo music downstairs went off leaving a loud silence. Hilary's eyes, wide with alarm, caught Alan's. He put his finger to his lips and nodded with his head for her to leave the room. Reaching down, he snapped off the lamp.

At the first step Hilary took the floor creaked as though it were splitting in half.

"Oh my God," she whispered, and meant it.

Alan's silhouette glided through the shadows. He made no more noise than the cat itself as he went to the front windows, pulling the shade back a fraction.

He swore softly staring down at the dome-shaped head shining baldly in the porch light. Voices floated up.

"*Wait!*"

Alan's urgent whisper stopped Hilary with her hand on the front door knob.

"Lock it."

Fingers fumbling, she obeyed, sliding the dead-bolt home.

"It's our friend from Scotland Yard."

"How can that be? Is he following us?" *I'm going to jail,* she thought numbly. *I'm going to jail for a thousand years.*

At her feet the cat mewed to be let out. Alan moved past Hilary into the kitchen. She heard the window sash scrape as he inched it open.

"Hilary." His whispered command had Hilary joining him at the open window. Staring down at the tiny patch of lawn, she checked out the flimsy trellis entwined with roses. The night air was heavy with smog, rain and wet roses. Hilary listened to the soft patter of raindrops hitting leaves.

She ducked her head back inside the window.

"Alan, there is no way."

"There's no choice."

"It's an eighteen foot drop!"

"Nearer twenty, so don't fall."

From the front came the clomp of heavy feet on the wooden stairway like storm-troopers on the march. Hilary threw one leg over the windowsill and hesitated, feeling her foot swing out into nothingness.

"*Go,*" said Alan. He started to push her through the open window.

Hilary clutched at the window frame. "I can't! There's nothing to hold on to!"

"God damn it—"

"Don't take the Lord's name in vain!"

At this fraught moment Xeres' cat chose to come pussy-footing onto the window sill ignoring the human commotion there and fanning its tail in Hilary's face as it sniffed the air inquiringly.

Alan muttered under his breath, scooped the cat up and dropped it over the sill. The cat went down the trellis with a yowl, claws scrabbling at leaves and vine.

"Alan!"

"You're next." Alan put one hand on the back of Hilary's head, guiding her under the sash.

Just for an instant Hilary recognized something familiar in this mechanical motion, but the thought vanished as she found herself dangling twenty feet above the ground.

Alan hissed, "Feel with your foot. There are wooden pegs in the trellis. Xeres meant this thing as an escape route."

Hilary felt around with her foot. Alan was right. There were wooden pegs strategically placed within the vines of the trellis.

"Bloody hell. *Go!*"

Behind them Hilary heard the sound of a key in the front door. She felt for the next peg, hanging to the edge of the slippery windowsill. Her arms shook. Hilary was a fit girl but this Tarzan and Jane stuff was a bit more strenuous than she was used to.

Dimly she was aware that Alan had ducked back into the apartment. Biting back her instinctive protest, Hilary stretched for the next foothold. She groped through the leaves for something to hang on to and shifted her other foot. One more peg down she decided she was close enough to the ground to risk jumping.

Her descent dislodged the cat, which was scaling back up the trellis. The cat fell with another screech of protest, somehow catching itself in Hilary's clothing with twenty separate needle-sharp claws.

Hilary landed in the wet grass with a jar that sent pain shooting up her ankles through her shinbones to her teeth.

From above came a loud crash followed by the sound of broken glass and a thud that seemed to shake the duplex. Briefly Alan appeared framed in the dark window, knee up, hands braced against the frame.

Picking herself up, Hilary ran, shoes squelching, trying to dislodge the still clinging cat. She darted around the corner, scrabbling for her keys with one hand, with the other swatting at the persistent feline who had sunk its claws in and was hanging on for dear life. Maybe someday—if she wasn't arrested—she would see the humor in the situation. At the moment it felt like Job's night out.

Hauling open the Renault door, she finally succeeded in plucking off the cat which immediately twisted out of her grasp and leaped into the back seat. The cat was the least of her worries. Hilary jabbed the key in the ignition and the engine roared into life in a way that would have given Selena second thoughts about loaning her car out.

The next instant Alan yanked open the passenger door and jumped in beside her. Hilary squealed away from the curb.

"Turn left," Alan ordered.

Hand over hand, Hilary swung a tight left.

"Left again."

"Do you know where we're going?" she asked even as she followed his instructions. It occurred to Hilary that her driving skills were improving dramatically by the second.

"Pull up in this driveway. Cut the engine. Lights."

Hands unsteady, Hilary turned into a driveway, jerking to a stop. She turned off the engine and the lights.

"Down." Alan's hand on her head pushed Hilary lower in her seat.

They waited in silence. Hilary could hear her wrist watch, the rain on the metal roof, and the soft fast sound of Alan's breathing. There was no sound of pursuit. No cars. No sirens.

The minutes ticked by.

"Meow," complained a voice from the back.

***

"Is it just me?" Hilary inquired, after San Francisco's lights had vanished into the mist behind them. "Or are things getting more complicated by the minute?"

Alan grunted tired concurrence, absently stroking the cat, which was purring contentedly on his lap. The sight of Alan with the cat he swore was not his brought a smile to Hilary's mouth, but she persisted in her line of reasoning.

"Obviously Lord Henry's death and the theft of his Rembrandt have something to do with all this—and if you say 'elementary' again, I'll slug you."

"I would agree that Lord Henry's murder is pivotal."

"Either Napier didn't expect to have his room searched or he wanted someone to find that portfolio. He sure didn't make a serious attempt to hide it."

"Napier never considered that his room would be searched. He didn't anticipate dying."

Alan's voice sound tired and flat. He had not been himself since they walked into Napier's hotel room, Hilary thought. Briefly she glanced from the rain-blurred windshield and the road snaking blackly ahead. She knew her concern would not be welcome. She said instead, "If you notice, all those thefts were from private collections. Every case clipping had to do with individual collectors. No museums. No galleries."

"Right. So?"

"So we're not talking major thefts really. I mean, nothing on the scale of *The Nightwatch,* for example. Not that one and a half million pounds is chump change, but it seems to me that it would take something more than dollar signs to turn someone from Napier's background."

"We don't have any proof that Napier was a bent copper. That has always been speculation. Frankly, from the look of that portfolio, I'd surmise he was over here poking his beak into something he hadn't the go ahead on."

"Can we assume each of those case clippings is connected? That the thief or thieves is the same person in each instance?"

"Possibly."

"What I don't get is where the forgery comes in. Why does a thief need a forger? He's *got* the painting."

This was the question teasing Alan's brain. If it hadn't been for that single cutting concerning the de-frauded Japanese collector he would have been willing to abandon the forgery theory entirely. Steeple Hill's connection to the case might have been coincidence or speculation, but that solitary incident of a forged painting amidst all those stolen originals changed the case complexion utterly. As far as Alan was concerned, forgery conclusively tied in Steeple Hill's artists.

"Maybe the forged paintings are to replace the stolen paintings?" Hilary's eyes were trained on the slick road ahead.

"But that never happened. The only instance of forgery was that Manet in Hamamoto's collection."

"That we know of."

THE ART OF DYING

"Did you want me to drive?" Alan asked as she swerved widely to miss a fallen branch.

"No, I want you to use your brilliant powers of deductive reasoning," Hilary retorted. "This is good experience for me."

Alan said something Hilary couldn't make out.

"What was that?"

"Nothing."

"What if," Hilary posed, "the Manet *was* stolen, originally, I mean."

"You mean Hamamoto knowingly buys a hot Manet? He'd have had it examined and authenticated even so."

"But what if it was genuine?"

Alan's eyes narrowed. "You're suggesting a genuine Manet might have been stolen and sold, with a forged copy substituted at the last minute?"

"Yes! They pull a switch. It's possible right? Unscrupulous collectors do knowingly buy stolen paintings."

"An art scam?" Alan mused.

A large chunk of the puzzle dropped into place. It would be so simple really: choice pieces stolen in publicized crimes and then sold a couple of times over because forgeries had been made for each theft. Two or three copies of the original painting could be sold at a couple of million pounds per. They wouldn't need to steal the *Mona Lisa* with that kind of profit margin.

"It's perfect," Hilary enthused. "They could sell the genuine article to whichever buyer seemed the most potentially dangerous or the most lucrative in the long run. And it would all be hush-hush because the paintings *are* stolen. If the fraud were to be discovered the victim couldn't exactly run to the police."

"There are other means of retaliation."

"Sure, but these people are crooks. They must have means of protecting themselves. And they probably hand-picked their victims to minimize risk."

"It's plausible," Alan conceded.

"It's more than plausible. And it makes much more sense that

Napier would gamble his career for stakes like these. His cut could be a million pounds in non-taxable income per theft, depending on how many people are involved in the scam."

"But he'd have to account for that kind of money."

"On his W-2 form? Be serious. He came from a wealthy family. He was a lord or something."

"Baronet," objected Alan. "That doesn't mean he was a millionaire."

"You saw his belongings. A sterling silver shaving mug? Not silver plate. The thing had a hallmark."

"Hilary—"

Having got her attention at last Alan could think of no more powerful argument than, "You're jumping to conclusions. We've got to think it through logically. These people are dangerous."

"I realize that," Hilary said, unperturbed, shifting gears as they began their downhill descent. "Maybe Napier was trying to double-cross them and they killed him. We still don't know where you fit into this. I don't believe you had anything to do with Lord Henry's murder simply because you sort of remember being there. For all we know Napier killed him."

Alan shook his head.

Hilary continued stubbornly, "After all, Lord Henry used to work for Scotland Yard. That can't be a coincidence. There's a definite tie-in. Perhaps Lord Henry was on to Napier?"

"We don't know Napier wasn't here investigating Lord Henry's murder."

"*Here?* Why would he hunt for the killer here when Lord Henry was killed over there?"

"Because the killer may be over here."

She knew who Alan thought the murderer was, who Napier had been chasing in sunny California. "Why are you defending the guy?"

"I'm not. I hated the bastard, but . . ." Alan's voice trailed as he recalled that dream, sitting in the interrogation room across from Napier. For an instant he had a sensation of light-headedness as though some pressure in his head shifted, tilted. He shut his eyes. When he re-opened them the world had righted itself. The moment of dizziness was past.

"Do you know something else? We don't know you killed Napier. You blacked out. Maybe it was for longer than you realize. Maybe Alan Xeres came in, in the meantime—"

"Watch a lot of telly, do you?"

"I don't even own a TV."

"Then you have a frighteningly fertile imagination. Xeres could not get in and out of that house without the taxi driver seeing him."

"You did."

"Hilary, dear girl, think it through," Alan said exasperatedly. "Why would Xeres not kill me as well as Napier? Why wouldn't he take the money and note addressed to himself? And where is Xeres now? If I'm his partner or confederate why hasn't he contacted me?"

"He doesn't know where you are."

"Then he can't be looking very hard."

"Maybe he isn't looking very hard for a reason."

Alan sighed a long sigh of strained patience.

"Okay, try this," Hilary said. "Maybe he's lying low too."

"What?"

"Hiding out."

"Yes, I know what it means." Alan fell silent watching her hands moving capably on the steering wheel. She had small hands with slim brown fingers and neatly clipped nails. He studied her hands in the dashboard light and thought he could recollect other hands: soft, white hands with manicured nails. Hands designed for wearing jewels or toasting champagne glasses or expertly pleasuring a man. Whose hands? The thought of Hilary's thin, warm hands stroking his body was incredibly erotic. Alan had to elbow this mental image aside.

Shifting the sleeping cat, he settled more comfortably in his seat. His headache, which had never quite left him from the moment of waking up in an abandoned house in a foreign country, was returning full force. He felt drained, depressed. He listened to the beat and swish of the windscreen blades and wished Hilary would stop chattering. Wished that she would stop poking and prying with that fox terrier tenacity.

Shut your mouth and let me love. Who had said that, or something close to that? Not that he loved Hilary, for Christ's sake. He remembered her panicked reproof of, 'Don't take the Lord's name in vain,' right before he shoved her out the window, and a faint smile curved his mouth.

Hilary's voice broke into the long silence, jerking Alan back into wakefulness.

"Why don't we try some free association?" she suggested. "You know, I say a word and you tell me what it makes you think of. Your gut reaction."

His gut reaction to that proposal was a speeding up of his heart rate and a sinking in the aforementioned gut. He managed to say indifferently, "If it will help pass the drive for you."

"Yes, it will." Hilary chewed her lip thoughtfully. ""Cat."

"Dog."

She turned her head briefly. "What kind of dog? Try to be specific."

"I don't know. What kind of dog? Border collie. Black and white. Freckles."

"Home."

"London."

"Be more—"

"Right. Er . . . traffic then. Rain. St. James Park. Pint of Bass. Stone lions. Georgian brick . . ." Alan shook his head as though off-balance. He wondered if Hilary carried any aspirin in her outsized bag of tricks.

"Wife."

"Ball and chain."

Hilary laughed. "I should tape this for future blackmail. Mother."

"Grey silk."

"Come again?"

Alan shrugged. "Grey silk frock, I suppose. This is pointless."

"Father."

"Funeral. Police." The irritation was gone from Alan's voice. "Black. Gold buttons, braid." Alan put a hand to his head. Images flashed through his mind like scenes glimpsed from a train window: a woman with milky skin and blue-rinsed hair, a white house in the country. It was all muddled. He could feel a cold sweat starting out all over his body. Why the *hell* couldn't she leave it alone?

"You seem fixated on fashion details. Picasso."

"Over-rated."

Hilary chuckled again. He liked her laugh. He relaxed a little.

"Thief."

"Catch."

"Painter."

"Thief."

"Alan—"

"Dead."

Hilary swerved sharply, the Renault's tires spraying water in a sheet. She risked a glance at Alan. In the ghostly light of the dashboard she could see his forehead wrinkled with pain or thought.

"Napier?" she asked in a whisper of a voice.

"Guilty." The word came out fiercely.

Hilary's unease grew. "Alan," she began again.

"Blood. Hands . . ."

"Alan!" Quickly Hilary pulled off to the side of the road and cut the engine. Rain rattled down on the roof of the car deafeningly as she turned to Alan. "Alan, are you all right? Can you hear me?"

His hands felt like ice. His was breathing hard as though he had been sprinting through a particularly dark and stormy night. He said at last, as though her words had finally sunk in, "Right-o." His voice sounded creaky, as though he hadn't used it in years.

"Of course you're all right or of course you hear me?"

She wanted to make him talk, wanted to force him to think, to move away from wherever there was blood on his hands.

"I'm fine." If his voice hadn't been ever so slightly shaky it would have sounded irritable.

"I'm sorry."

"For what?"

For jabbing her mop in the cobwebbed corners of his mind? "For playing amateur psychologist. I have no idea what I'm doing. I don't want to confuse your actual memories. Who knows if this kind of thing could make your amnesia worse? Maybe your inability to remember isn't physical. After all, you weren't hurt that badly. The bruise is fading. What if this is some kind of psychological amnesia? What if you saw something that day?"

"Something that sent me into traumatic shock?" Alan sounded more like himself: sarcastic and skeptical. "Do I strike you as the fragile flower type?"

"Your machismo isn't at issue here."

"Look, dear girl, I've been in fights before. I've seen dead bodies before. Don't ask me how I know, I just do. Nothing that happened in that house sent me off the deep end."

Dear girl? Was that an improvement over 'luv?' "How do you know? You don't remember everything that happened."

"I *know*."

"The king has spoken."

"I know," he repeated, with unshakable finality.

***

The rain had softened to silvery mist by the time they drove into Steeple Hill. The chapel bell chimed the half-hour as the Renault wound through the sparkling streets. Diamond drops glittered from the gingerbread eaves and spangled the leafy branches over-hanging Stevenson Street.

"Pretty," Alan commented noncommittally.

Hilary nodded agreement. She loved Steeple Hill at night. With the old-fashioned street lights burning, the lamps glowing behind lace curtains in the renovated houses she could see the Steeple Hill of a half-century before when it had been a simple fishing village. The sort of place Grace May North would have written about in the books Hilary had read as a girl.

"Is half-ten too late to pay a call on Bryan?" Alan asked breaking the tired silence that had fallen between them.

They had switched places the last leg of the trip, and now Hilary directed Alan to Bryan's house, a small back street rental with waist-high weeds in the yard and a beat-out orange van parked in front. There were lights on behind all the curtains and the front door stood open.

Alan followed Hilary as she picked her way up the uneven path. She tapped on the doorframe. There was no response. Hilary poked her head into the room.

Bryan sat on a low stool sketching madly with charcoals. Sitting Indian-style on the floor across from him was one of the loveliest girls Alan had ever seen. She was tall and slender with hair like liquid gold spilling over her shoulders, and delicate, cameo-like features. Her eyes were huge gentian-blue. They shimmered with tears that welled and trickled unheeded down her satin cheeks.

Neither Bryan nor his companion seemed to hear Hilary's knock.

"Just tell Tom, baby. Just lay it on the line." Bryan's clever fingers sketched away, capturing the moment.

"What if I'm wrong? He'll never forgive me," wept the girl.

"You're not wrong," Bryan said indifferently. "Shit, everyone knows what's going on."

Hilary knocked again and Bryan jumped to his feet nearly oversetting the three-legged stool.

"Hilary, hey!" His smile was wide and forced. "And . . . uh . . . what was your name?"

"Alan." Alan gave the room a sweeping glance that encompassed all its second-hand shabbiness. Art paraphernalia was strewn everywhere.

The girl rose dashing tears away, showing the first signs of self-consciousness.

"Hi, Hilary," she gulped.

"Hi, Mary." After the briefest hesitation Hilary said, "Alan, this is Mary Campbell, Steeple Hill's most popular model."

"Are you being snide?" Bryan inquired.

"Why would I be?"

Bryan shrugged.

Mary looked at her watch. "I've got to go." She grabbed a hooded poncho from the hook behind the door and edged past Hilary and Alan with a breathy, "Excuse me."

Her hurried footsteps disappeared down the walk.

Bryan shoved his sketch pad aside and stood up. "This *is* an honor. What can I do for you, Hilary?" He wandered into the kitchen, pulled open the humming refrigerator and held up half a bottle of rosé.

Hilary shook her head no, Alan, however nodded, and Bryan's face brightened.

"We were looking for a friend of yours, Bryan," Hilary began.

"Oh yeah? Who's that?"

"Alan Xeres."

Bryan poured the wine into fruit jars and handed one to Alan. "Haven't seen him in months." He knocked his own back as though doing shots. "What the hell happened to your hands?" he asked suddenly, coming up for air.

Hilary glanced down at her hands. The backs were red with cuts and scratches from the combination of cat and rose thorns. Nothing requiring a doctor, but noticeable. Now that Bryan mentioned it, they were stinging quite a bit too.

"I—uh—got a cat today," she offered lamely.

"What kind, mountain lion?" Bryan headed back for the kitchen where he pulled a surprisingly clean first aid kit out of a drawer. He tossed it over the counter to Hilary. "Think fast."

Hilary caught the kit with a mutter of thanks, opened it and sprayed her hands with Bactine.

"You ought to have those babies insured."

At the edge in Bryan's voice, Alan looked from Hilary to Bryan. "I'm surprised Pauley hasn't insisted."

Hilary said nothing. She finished disinfecting her hands.

"The hands are everything. Next to the eyes."

"Yeah. Thanks."

"So why are you looking for Xeres?" Bryan questioned, leaning back against the counter.

Alan responded, "I thought he might know something about a friend of mine I'm trying to locate."

Hilary noticed the newspaper lying on the end of the counter. Alex Napier's face stared up at her. With that long hair and beard he could more easily have passed for Jesus than a cop. A thought occurred to Hilary. What did a man with a full beard need with a shaving mug?

"Yeah, well it'll cost you. I never knew Xeres to give anything away, including information." Bryan took another gulp of wine and swished it through his teeth. He said sadly, "I shouldn't drink. I can't hold the stuff. I've got this chemical imbalance thing."

There seemed to be nothing to say to that. The three of them listened to the rain drumming on the roof and splashing off the stoop outside the open door. There were canvases everywhere. Stacks of unsaleable paintings. The room reeked of paint and turps, of cooked cabbage, of poverty and defeat.

Bryan said, "Serena's the one you should talk to. She was seeing Xeres for awhile. I think they still keep in touch." He added gloomily, "Bastard."

"Who?" asked Hilary.

"Xeres. He knew how I felt about her." Bryan sighed heavily. "Everyone knows how I feel about her."

Alan drained his glass and set it on the counter.

"'Nother?" Bryan asked hopefully.

"Not for me, no. Thanks."

"Hil?"

"No thanks, Bry."

Bryan's face puckered up. "Hilary, won't you talk to Grainger for me? He'd listen to you. It's not fair . . ." His brown eyes had that teary look again. "Holier-than-thou Grainger Pauley. You know, Becca's told me a few stories about Grainger and the good old days."

"I'll talk to him," Hilary promised.

"Would you do that? Would you?"

"Yes."

Bryan drained his second glass of wine and banged the fruit glass on the counter. "I feel like painting," he announced.

***

"Serena is not your forger," Hilary said as Alan slid under the steering wheel and put the key to the ignition.

"Did I say she was?"

"I saw your eyes light up. You looked like something on *Wild Kingdom* when it spots its prey."

Alan was silent. They watched the rain trickle down the windshield in rivulets like Mary Campbell's tears.

"Hilary," he said at last, "I can't back away from this. It's not only my life at stake, it's yours as well. And I'd rather have you alive and well and hating my guts than . . . have something happen to you."

Hilary swallowed. "I'm not asking you to back off. I know it's too late for that. But I know Serena is not a criminal."

"Because she's your friend?"

"No, because it would be a stupid risk. The Thomases already earn an excellent living from the shop."

"Have you seen their account books?"

"Of course not."

"Then you assume they earn an excellent living."

"She designs jewelry. Serena is not a painter. Forgery is an art. It's not paint by numbers. Serena couldn't fake a Rembrandt if her life depended on it. You're talking about a particular degree of skill. Just because she dated Xeres a few times—you said yourself he had a little black book full of women's names. Was Serena's name in the book?"

"No. But it was an old directory. Ten years or more. That's why it was stuffed in the back of the drawer."

After a moment Hilary said huskily, "Besides, we already know they know each other." She picked up the cat and buried her face in the soft fur. She didn't want Alan to know how close she was to tears.

The cat wriggled out of her hold and scrambled over the seat. Hilary took a deep, steadying breath and stared out the window. She wished Alan would start driving.

Instead he turned the engine off.

"Listen," he began.

She listened but he said nothing. Then to Hilary's astonishment Alan put his arm around her shoulder, pulling her against him despite the emergency brake and gear box.

Hilary was too surprised to say anything for a moment. Hr face was pressed into Alan's broad shoulder, which smelt of soap and rain and man.

"I am sorry," Alan murmured against her ear. "I'm sorry you were ever involved in this. I wouldn't hurt you for the world." His fingers massaged the base of her skull, soothing the tension knotting her spine. He was offering comfort, Hilary warned herself. Nothing more, nothing less.

She gave a shiver as Alan placed one tiny, velvet kiss in the hollow beneath her ear.

"God, you smell good. You taste good."

"Thank you," Hilary managed in a slightly strangled voice.

His hands smoothed over her shoulders as though he were trying to make up his mind.

"Hilary?"

"Huh?"

One of Alan's hands began to work the buttons of her denim shirt. The next instant his hand had slipped in and was caressing her breast through the wisp of lace bra.

Hilary moaned as Alan's thumb traced the outline of her nipple.

"You *feel* so good," he muttered. He pressed the palm of his hand against Hilary's breast, rubbing until her breast stood up full and swollen.

Hilary mentally opened and shut drawers full of words she couldn't bring herself to use. She sighed then gasped as Alan caressed her other breast. It seemed as though she had waited for this from the moment she had laid eyes on him waiting in the hot sun for the bus to Steeple Hill. It seemed as though she had been waiting for this for years.

She wanted him to take her right now, right in the car in Bryan's driveway. The shock of that thought brought a glimmer of sanity to Hilary's fevered brain.

"Alan," she gulped as Alan's mouth found her own. "Alan, wait," she pleaded.

With unflattering promptness she was released. Hilary opened her mouth, had no idea of what to say, and closed it again, her fingers automatically doing up the buttons on her shirt. She felt for the straps of her seat belts as though seeking restraint from an outside source.

Alan raked a hand through his hair, then started the Renault's engine, pausing to mop at the clouded windshield with his handkerchief. The windows were completely steamed up, and a nervous giggle escaped Hilary.

Alan's eyes slid to hers. He laughed unwillingly.

***

There was no sign of the Thomases as Alan and Hilary climbed the stairs to the flat, although Hilary spied a band of light beneath their door and heard the shimmer of sitar music as they passed.

She unlocked the apartment and switched on the fan-shaped lights.

"I'll make tea." When in doubt, make tea.

From the kitchen Hilary watched the gray cat prowl the loft, the tip of his tail twitching suspiciously. Alan sat at the table idly rolling a pencil back and forth. Surreptitiously he watched Hilary watching him. All day since they had stood in Napier's hotel room he had felt his old life overshadowing the present. Memory was there, hovering like the bright aura that comes with migraine.

"What am I supposed to do with this cat?" Hilary inquired. "Do you suppose the police will add cat-napping to all the other charges?"

"In this bloody country it probably carries the highest penalty of all."

"I wonder if the mysterious Mr. X will want him back."

Alan's reply was forestalled by a faint scratching at the door. He went to answer it.

One of the Thomases stood there. Bright perfect mouth, so it was Selena. The graphic artist. The one who managed the books.

Her smile was perfunctory. "Hi, Alan. Is Hilary—?" She looked past him to the kitchen and Hilary. "Hi, Hil," she called. "Serena needs the car tomorrow, if that's okay?"

"Sure. Thanks for letting us borrow it."

"No problem." Selena watched the cat weave around Alan's legs without comment. She seemed to have something else on her mind.

"Did you want a cup of tea?" Hilary invited, carrying the pot over to the table.

"What? No." Selena seemed to make up her mind. "Hil, the police were here today."

"The police? Really?" Hilary was careful to avoid looking Alan's way.

"That's what he said. A big grizzled guy. He said his name was Hogsworth and that he was from Scotland Yard. I don't think he has any jurisdiction here, but if *he* knows then our own sheriff's department must know."

"Must know what?" Alan questioned.

Selena cast him a level look.

"Why should you think we have anything to hide?" Alan persisted.

"I don't think Hilary does," Selena told him. "I think he was looking for *you*. There's a description in the evening paper of the man a shuttle bus driver claims boarded his bus near Seal Point the afternoon that Scotland Yard detective was murdered. This man paid for his fare with a hundred dollar bill."

"Sounds like someone deliberately trying to bring attention to himself."

Selena grew impatient. "He said this man was tall, thin and dark-haired; in his mid-thirties. He said he wore jeans and white shirt and that he had very pale green eyes. He remembered the eyes particularly."

"Glowing as they no doubt did with a murderous light," mocked Alan.

Selena tossed her rippling mane. "Go ahead and laugh," she retorted, "but I know it was you on that bus. It's too big a coincidence. You never fell down any flight of stairs. You must have been in a fight with that English cop."

"You think I killed him?" Alan was smiling but it was not a friendly effort, Hilary thought.

"I don't care one way or the other," Selena said flatly. "But Hilary's my friend and she deserves to know."

"Did Grainger put you up to this?" Hilary asked.

"What does Grainger have to do with it? Come to think of it he did say he thought there was something fishy about Alan." Selena looked thoughtful. "Maybe you're right. Maybe he sent that Hogsworth here."

"Thanks for the warning," Hilary told her.

Selena glanced at Alan and shrugged. "Sorry, Alan, but . . ."

"Don't sweat it. Did you promise to call this bloke from Scotland Yard if I turned up?"

"Yes." Selena went towards the door. "But I didn't say when. I'll wait till morning."

"Thanks."

Avoiding Hilary's eyes Selena turned, closing the door softly behind her.

CHAPTER NINE

Hilary's eyes flew to Alan's. "What now?"

"Will she keep her word?"

"About waiting till morning? Yes."

Alan rubbed the back of his neck. "Then I suggest we get some sleep."

"*Sleep?*"

He raised his eyebrows. "What did you have in mind?"

"Don't we need to do something? Make plans?"

Alan put his arms around Hilary, pulling her to him, holding her close for a moment.

"You're leaving, aren't you?" She listened to the steady beat of his heart.

Alan—she still thought of him as Alan—didn't answer. His cheek rested briefly on the top of her head.

"You're going to leave me to face the police," Hilary added bitterly.

Alan's head lifted. His fingers bit into her shoulders as he met her gaze. "You know why I'm leaving."

"Then why can't I go with you?"

This was followed by a mutually flabbergasted silence.

"Go with me where, luv?" Alan was staring at Hilary as though she had lost her mind. He gave a half-laugh. "To prison? Or do you fancy life on the run?"

It *was* mad. She had no idea why she had suggested it. But Hilary wished that Alan could at least have considered it for a split second. She directed her irritation elsewhere.

"Don't call me 'luv.' I am not your love."

Alan's expression was wry. "Aren't you? I'd rather begun to think of you that way."

Hilary's heart leapt. She turned away, Alan's hands falling from her shoulders. "I thought you were afraid you were already married?"

"That is a possibility, isn't it?" He sighed sounding more weary than he had in all their time together.

Neither spoke for a moment. Then Alan added, as though it were a matter of indifference, "I can't imagine I could care for someone else and still feel this way about you. That's probably naiveté on my part."

The hope that Hilary had firmly damped down sprang into a full roaring fire. She turned back to Alan, blue eyes shining like jewels.

"Are you serious?"

"It doesn't change anything," he warned.

"No, I suppose not."

"Then why are you smiling?"

"You're not much of an optimist are you?"

"No." But Alan gently pulled her back into his arms. "Let me lie with you tonight, Hilary," he whispered.

"Alan—"

"I want one night—tonight—to hold against all the other nights."

To deny him was to double her own pain.

"I am an optimist," Hilary told him, "but even I can see that one or both of us may end up in prison. We may never see each other again. Or maybe when you get your memory back you won't remember *me*. I saw that in a movie once."

Alan grinned wryly. "*Random Harvest*. I saw it too. That won't happen. That much I guarantee."

Hilary said softly, "You can't make guarantees. I know that."

Their eyes held for a moment.

"I don't want you to regret this," Alan said roughly.

Hilary smiled. "I think I'll regret it more if we spend the rest of this night talking."

***

The secret things belong to our God.

They lay together in the soft blankets listening to the rain. The watery blackness outside the Palladian windows gave the rooms an underwater feel, Hilary thought fancifully, as though they were in Captain Nemo's Nautilus 20,000 leagues below.

This moment in time was theirs alone. And nothing that came after could change that, she reflected, as Alan's mouth once more moved leisurely on her own. She was a thirty-year old woman, not a child, and she made her own choices. And lived with the consequences. She had not expected to feel guilt, but she was surprised at how *right* this felt. It felt as natural as though they had been making love to each other for years, as though they were man and wife; two halves of a spiritual whole. She opened her mouth, tasting Alan.

Hilary would have guessed that Alan was man who used sex as an outlet; a man who shunned the emotional intimacy of the act. If he couldn't actually leave, she would have expected him to with-draw after a well-bred interval to his own side of the bed. But Alan showed no sign of going anywhere. Between kisses his chest rose and fell tranquilly against her back, his hand lazily stroked her skin.

"Are you sleeping?" he asked after a long time.

"No."

"I don't want to sleep tonight," Alan said dreamily. "I don't want to waste a moment of this night. I want to make love to you again and again."

Hilary grinned in the darkness. "Ambitious aren't you?"

"Mmmhmm." He leaned over and nuzzled her ear. "If I doze off wake me up. Poke me in the ribs or something."

Hilary murmured, "Or something." She felt the laugh that rumbled in his chest.

They lay in a comfortable tangle of blankets, legs and arms. The rain slackened and began again. Hilary's thoughts wandered afar.

"Alan?"

"Mmm?" His head jerked slightly and Hilary smiled, knowing he had been on the edge of sleep. His arms tightened around her.

"How old was that photo of Napier?"

"I don't know."

"Did he look like he looked in that photo? Did he have that beard?"

"No, he was clean-shaven."

"But if it was a passport photo?"

"A passport photo can be something like seven years old." Alan smothered a yawn. "What's the time?"

"Nearly one o'clock. Was his hair—"

"I don't want to talk about Napier. Tonight let's not think about Napier or Xeres or any of it. Let it be you and me and no tomorrow."

It was such an uncharacteristically romantic thing for Alan to say it gave Hilary pause. "Well, I'll try," she mumbled. "It won't be easy but I'll do my—"

Alan silenced her with a kiss.

When she came up for air Hilary said, "I knew the first moment I laid eyes on you you'd be a great kisser."

"Years of practice."

"I don't want to hear about it."

"I couldn't tell you if I wanted to," he pointed out. "For me this is my first time. There's nothing and no one to compare to it. I don't suppose anything could stand the comparison."

Hilary reached up, her fingertips felt the roughness of his jaw, starting the next day's beard. Their time was fleeting, she thought. She said, "Gallantly put. You *have* had practice."

"My body would remember anything this . . ."

"Significant?" teased Hilary. "Earth-shattering?"

Alan's hand slid up finding her breast. His thumb brushed her nipple and the cinders cooling inside Hilary sparked into wakefulness. "Of course I can only speak for myself."

Hilary eased on to her back. "Fishing for compliments?" Her

hand fondled him feeling Alan's arousal stand to attention like a small, eager soldier. "You weren't kidding about all night, were you?"

"No."

"I want you to try some free association." Alan's lazy drawl drew Hilary back into wakefulness.

"Me?" she protested, reluctantly letting go of cozy oblivion. Was it her imagination or was the room already lighter? The rain had stopped. The darker shadows of the furniture stood out in the gloom. Hilary could just make out Alan's features.

"Okay, shoot." She sighed, her eyes closing once more.

"Sex." Alan's index finger slid down the bony ridge of her spine.

"Love," she gulped, arching away from that teasing touch.

"How feminine." Alan drew her back against his body, folding his arm beneath her breasts. "Scotland Yard."

"Sherlock Holmes."

"Sherlock Holmes didn't work for Scotland Yard."

"Whose associations are these?" She tilted her chin, listening for his answer.

"Sherlock Holmes."

"Moriarity."

"Hm. Painting."

"Steal."

"We're getting into trouble here." Alan was amused.

"Do you remember how you broke your nose?" Hilary asked, turning to study Alan's face. Yes, it was definitely getting lighter. She could make out the color of his eyes, green as an English spring.

She was surprised when he answered, his voice sleepy. "A sailboat when I was a kid. The boom swung around and I forgot to duck."

Alan didn't notice that he had remembered anything and Hilary was careful to avoid any outward show of excitement. Alan's memory was coming back so gradually he hadn't realized it yet. It was probably only a matter of days before he remembered everything.

She wanted to trace his features with her fingertips; to memorize every arrogant, beautiful bone in his face, the black wings of his eyebrows, the curve of his sexy mouth. It was harder in the daylight, she felt almost shy.

"Painting," Alan offered.

"Forgery."

There was a pause. With her eyes shut once more Hilary queried, "Still think I'm knocking off Old Masters?"

"I never did truly." Alan's voice grew grave. "If it seemed that way, forgive me. I—er—haven't quite been myself lately."

Hilary raised one lid and gave a sleepy giggle.

***

When she opened her eyes again Alan was gone.

The loft felt quiet and empty in a way it never had before she met Alan. Hilary reached out and the sheets were still warm where his body had lain.

He didn't say good-bye, she thought achingly, but was instantly struck by the silliness of that. Alan had said good-bye in every imaginable way last night. Her body still felt the imprint of his.

She said a simple prayer asking God to watch over Alan.

Something light landed on the foot of the bed. Hilary raised her head over the white edge of the sheet and met the intense green gaze of Alan Xeres's cat. It approached on belly, apparently planning to jump her.

"Hi Cat," Hilary said.

The cat opened its wide pink mouth and meowed. A big meow for such a little cat.

"You have a one track mind." Hilary sat up. For perhaps the first time in her life she felt apathetic at the start of a new day.

Pushing the bedclothes aside she padded into the kitchen followed by the cat. There was no sign to show Alan had ever been in her quarters. He had removed every trace of himself. Even the pencil he had toyed with last night was neatly replaced in a jar on the counter. Knowing Alan, Hilary thought wryly, he had probably wiped all his fingerprints away too.

She turned on the teakettle, fed the cat half a can of salmon and sat down at the table staring down the long empty room of the loft.

I don't even know his real name, she thought. She pushed a hand through her hair then rose, fetching her sketchpad and pencils. She closed her eyes trying to recall the shape of his eyes, his not quite straight nose, that stubborn chin. Hilary opened her eyes. Her fingers began to sketch, her hand rapidly covered the page.

The heavy knock on her door broke Hilary's concentration. Grumbling she tossed the sketchpad aside and went to answer the door.

Impatience gave way to alarm at the sight of the big, soldierly man in the beautifully tailored suit on her threshold. Hilary's wide eyes took in thinning gray hair, a handlebar mustache, and unexpectedly kind brown eyes.

"Detective-Sergeant Hogsworth, Scotland Yard," the man said crisply, and offered her a flash of official-looking ID.

Hilary gaped and then gathered her wits.

"Scotland Yard?"

"May I come in, Miss Jackson?" Detective-Sergeant Hogsworth was coming in, in any case. Hilary moved aside automatically. Alarm bells were going off inside her head. *Keep your mouth shut,* she warned herself. She couldn't begin to know what was the wrong thing to say. To say as little as possible was her only hope.

Hogsworth emanated benign authority as he looked about her loft. "I understand you have an Englishman by the name of Allen staying with you, Miss?"

"Do you have any jurisdiction in this country, Sergeant Hogsworth?"

Scotland Yard never batted an eyelash. "If you prefer, I can have your local sheriff's department ask you to help with the inquiry, Miss Jackson."

Hilary thought that few things could make you feel more at a disadvantage than standing in your bathrobe and bare feet trying to face off a gigantic cop.

"I can't see why Scotland Yard would be interested in my house-guest—former house-guest, as you can see." Hilary strolled towards the table, flipped over the portrait of Alan and laid the pencils on top of it.

"We'd just like to ask him a few questions, Miss."

"About what?"

"Official business, Miss."

"Is this about that Scotland Yard Inspector, Napier? The one the newspapers are so full of?"

There was no answer. Uneasily Hilary glanced over her shoulder. The Sergeant was staring as Xeres' cat came slinking out from behind the kit hen counter. It wound itself around Hogsworth's immaculately shod feet. Apparently Xeres's cat was the least discriminating of felines.

"Hullo, Puss," the Sergeant said, stooping down to chuck the cat under the chin. When next the Sergeant's eyes met Hilary's they held an alert gleam she didn't like.

"What's his name, Miss?"

"His—? Oh, I just call him . . ." her eyes fell on the Monet Grainger had given her for her birthday. "Claude."

"Claude?" The sergeant's brows rose. "Had him long?"

"Oh, ages."

"Really? I wouldn't have put him much over a year old. Is Allen your friend's Christian name, Miss?"

The word 'Christian' threw her for some reason, out of context as it were.

"Christian and non-Christian," she answered like a dope, under the man's calm gaze. He had talked to Grainger. He had to know the answers before he asked the questions. She said defiantly, "Alan Allen. I've known him for years. Well, years ago. But he's gone back to Eng—Britain now. He left last night."

The sergeant straightened and Hilary had a sensation of a towering wall about to fall on her.

"Could you tell me what flight would that have been, Miss?"

"I'm not sure," Hilary faltered. "We said good-bye earlier."

"When and where was that?" Hilary could tell the sergeant was mentally licking a pencil and jotting it all down.

"In San Francisco. We had lunch at Tadich Grill. The cioppino, if you're interested. Then we said good-bye. I had some errands to run." What a huge mistake to give all these facts that could be disputed. For all she knew they hadn't been able to serve the cioppino yesterday because of an oyster shortage or something. Wasn't that how it worked on *Columbo?*

"What errands would those be, Miss?"

Hilary had been gearing up for questions about rental cars, how Alan had got to the airport, that kind of thing. Once again the unexpected turn threw her. She recognized that she had to stop this before she became tangled in her own lies.

"Why? Do I need an alibi? What happened yesterday that could possibly have to do with me?"

"Come come, Miss Jackson."

'Claude' feeling himself ignored, and with the manners one would expect from a crook's cat, meandered over and leaped atop the table. He landed on the sketch pad seesaw style and over-balanced it. The pad fell, fluttering loose pages to the floor like a wounded bird.

Hilary made a dive as sheets of paper went pin-wheeling everywhere. As bad luck would have it, the sketch of Alan floated to the floor, gliding to a stop at the toe of Detective-Sergeant Hogsworth's shoe.

As he stared down at it the sergeant's expression seemed to harden. Without a word he bent, retrieved the sheet and held it under Hilary's nose.

"Where did you get this, Miss?"

Hilary swallowed down her panic. "I drew it from a photo."

"What photo?"

"An old photo." Fear was making her stupid. Hilary could have bitten her tongue out for that last idiocy. The sergeant was shaking his head grimly.

"No, Miss. This was done recently. Where is he?"

"I don't know. That's the truth," Hilary said desperately.

Sergeant Hogsworth stared down at her form his Jovian height for a long moment. Then he said almost harshly, "You seem a nice girl, Miss. You couldn't draw like this and not have a caring heart. Maybe you've just got in too deep. But I'm warning you now, he's no friend of yours. He's let you in for murder. The murder of a police officer. Do you know what that means? Have you ever been in prison, Miss Jackson?"

Hilary's heart was pounding so hard her legs seemed to shake with it.

"What if it wasn't murder?" she got out. "What if it was an accident?"

"It was no accident. There's no accident about a man's head smashed to pulp. It's no accident that's taken out Alex Napier. I've known him all my life. I knew his father before him. And I'll tell you now, Miss, it'll be no accident what happens to those involved in his murder."

Hilary had to reach for the back of a chair to steady herself. She expected Hogsworth to whip out the handcuffs and arrest her on the spot. But Hogsworth just stood there waiting. Waiting for her to crack, Hilary gathered. Waiting for her to break down and confess and give Alan up to justice.

It dawned on Hilary that Hogsworth must not have the authority to arrest her or even threaten her. If he was working in conjunction with the sheriffs department why weren't the sheriffs with him now? And if he was not working with local law enforcement, he had no more authority than any other UK tourist. It began to look as though Hogsworth, like his chief before him, had a personal agenda.

If the sergeant wasn't working with the police, was he working around them? Just what was Hogsworth up to? How did he manage to keep turning up everywhere? How had he known to go to Grainger? Or to find Alan Xeres' apartment? Why *didn't* the sheriff's department seem to know what Hogsworth knew?

Hilary took a deep breath. "I've told you the truth," she said flatly. "Alan is gone. He never killed anyone. You're just wasting your time."

The sergeant took the portrait of Alan and folded the stiff paper in quarters. He slid it inside his suit jacket.

"Oh, I wouldn't say that, Miss," he informed Hilary grimly.

***

It didn't take Hilary more than ten minutes after closing the door on Detective Sergeant Hogsworth to get over to the gallery.

As usual Grainger was delighted to see her, settling Hilary in his leather-lined sanctum, plying her with offers of cappuccino and pastries.

"You set the police on Alan, didn't you?" she inquired coolly, when Grainger had finally seated himself behind the magnificent desk. "That Scotland Yard sergeant anyway," she qualified.

Grainger frowned. "That's hardly fair, my pet. I wasn't going to lie for him. I told you I thought he was a wrong 'un. But I didn't go to the police. They came to me."

"Why?"

Grainger looked momentarily confused. "Why? I'm not sure I follow."

Hilary thought Grainger followed her logic just fine. Grainger was the one who had implied, no, stated, he didn't believe Hilary knew Alan very well. Now he was trying to convince her that the police had approached him based on her long-standing relationship with Alan. He couldn't have it both ways and they both knew it.

Grainger shrugged. "I'm afraid the police didn't take me into their confidence, my pet. I'm sure they had their reasons for coming to me."

"I'm sure they did."

Grainger blinked and then smiled. "Now what does that mean?" He sounded indulgent, but Hilary thought she detected a certain steely glint in his pale blue eyes.

"Did you know Sir Alexander Napier thought the Pauley Galleries—and I—were involved in some kind of international art theft scam?"

Grainger had been sipping his cappuccino. Now he choked, spluttered and set the cup down with a bang. *"What?"*

It was one of the only times Hilary had heard him raise his voice.

"Who said—where did you—how—?" Grainger broke off as Hilary continued.

"The theory is that I'm forging repros of stolen Masters and you, under guise of the Pauley Galleries, are fencing them."

"That is absurd! Preposterous! Who told you that?"

Hard as she tried, Hilary couldn't detect anything beneath Grainger's justifiable outrage.

"No one has suggested any such thing to me. Who told you that?" fumed Grainger.

"Do you know a man named Alan Xeres?"

This time something did flicker in Grainger's eyes. "Someone named Xeres told you this?" he questioned sharply.

"Do you know who he is?" Hilary repeated, still ducking the direct question.

Grainger did not answer, leaning forward to light one of his expensive cigars. "Xeres?" he repeated, his uncharacteristic anger already evaporating. "Odd name. It does sound familiar. An artist?" He took a long meditative drag.

"I don't know. Maybe."

Grainger pinned her with a speculative eye. "Why are you so interested in him?"

An understandable question, but Hilary could hardly tell Grainger about the note addressed to A.X. and the wallet full of money that Alan had been carrying. Nor could she confide that Sir Alexander had had Xeres' phone number in his private papers, which Hilary had broken into a hotel room to examine.

She opened her mouth, but a stray thought crystallized in her brain.

Napier had been obsessed with Lord Henry's murder and the

theft of his Rembrandt to the extent that he had pursued his suspect across the Atlantic without official sanction. He had set up a meet with A.X., and A.X. or Alan Xeres had been paid four thousand dollars to get rid of Napier. That proved two things, didn't it? That Napier, who always did his homework, was certain Xeres was involved in Lord Henry Archibald's death; and that Xeres was deeply involved enough to risk killing a Scotland Yard inspector.

According to Alan, four thousand dollars wasn't enough money in itself; so there had to be some added incentive to make Xeres risk killing a cop. What? Hilary believed it had to be self-preservation because Napier was closing in. But not just on art theft and forgery. On murder. It was to conceal the first murder of Lord Henry, national hero and himself a former cop, that Xeres had been willing to commit the second: the murder of Sir Alexander Napier.

If Xeres had killed Lord Henry (could anything else justify the risk of killing Napier?) then Xeres had also stolen the Rembrandt and probably the other paintings in Napier's casebook. Hilary didn't think Xeres was the forger, given the painting she had seen in his apartment. He was certainly not the 'mastermind,' because that would be whoever had given Xeres the money to make himself scarce after killing Napier.

As Alan had pointed out, the man behind it all had to be someone with money and contacts within the art world, buyers and sellers both. Someone who had plenty to lose. Someone who was willing to risk (even at second hand) killing a cop, because discovery meant ruin.

Someone that ruthless had to be very dangerous when scared.

Hilary came out of her brown study to realized she hadn't answered Grainger.

"The sergeant mentioned him to me," she lied at random.

"Did he?" Grainger paused and puffed. "So was your young man arrested?"

"Why would he be? He hasn't done anything. He's gone back to England. He left yesterday."

"I see." Grainger continued to puff away. "Well, my pet," he said at last, "if I may give you some paternal advice, which I know you don't want, I suggest we put all this behind us and start focusing on next month's show."

"You're probably right." Hilary set her cup and saucer on the desk.

"I'm always right," Grainger told her imperturbably.

They chatted a while longer. Grainger seemed in no hurry to get rid of her, yet Hilary was aware that part of Grainger's mind was elsewhere. Perhaps running through the same mathematical process her own brain had.

And reaching the same conclusion?

They finished discussing the new show, and Hilary rose. "I meant to ask you about Bryan," she began.

"Now there is a coincidence," remarked Grainger glancing at his Rolex. "I'm having lunch with Bryan in about thirty minutes. A business lunch, otherwise I'd ask you to join us."

"Are you?" Hilary said quickly. "I'm glad. He really is gifted."

Grainger appeared amused. "Were you about to intercede on Bryan's behalf? He's a big boy, my pet. Well able to speak up for himself. I'd no idea you'd become so chummy with our resident problem child."

"We're not chummy. It's just . . ."

"Art," Grainger said succinctly. "Yes, I know. Which is why I'm willing to try one last time to talk sense. Dollars and sense."

***

Hilary walked out of the air-conditioned gallery into humid heat and an eerie kind of witch-light. Low clouds threatened, pressing down and smothering the town. The power lines above her head hummed; but the tension in the air was not all electrical, she decided.

What was that line in the Bible? *Then a spirit passed before my face; the hair of my flesh stood up.*

Yes, she thought. There was something in the air . . .

CHAPTER TEN

As she strolled along the tree-lined street Hilary had the crawly sensation of someone watching her. But a couple of casual glances over her shoulder offered no clue. The main street was busy, crowded with tourists and cars.

Hilary told herself that Detective-Sergeant Hogsworth was probably trailing her (not that he would be easy to miss), hoping she would lead him to Alan. Or perhaps the watching presence she felt was Alan himself? But no, if Alan had any sense at all he would be long gone by now. And one thing Alan had plenty of was sense.

The Campbells lived in a tiny A-frame on the beach. There was a waxed surfboard leaning against the house and an assortment of bathing suits drying on the line. A stained glass puffin hung in one window. Wind chimes tinkled softly in the breeze. Hilary knocked on the front door.

There was no answer.

She went round to the back. The Campbell's golden retriever barked a friendly invitation from inside the yard.

Hilary pounded on the back door.

No answer.

Nothing stirred inside the house.

Thoughtfully Hilary started back towards her own apartment.

Walking by Café Largo she heard someone calling her name. She spotted Becca sitting in the shady garden having lunch with one of the Thomas twins. By some coincidence Tom Campbell stood beside the table.

Becca waved Hilary over. "Come have dessert with us."

"Maybe an iced coffee," Hilary agreed, pulling a rattan chair over to the table.

"Sorry we missed your do the other night," Tom Campbell said. "Mary wasn't feeling well."

"Getting to be a habit, isn't it? Is she using, by any chance?"

Hilary glanced over at a black T-shirt and scarlet mouth: Selena. Naturally Selena. Serena never took that tone with anyone.

"No, she is not using!" Tom sounded annoyed. He was a handsome man, forty-something with curly black hair, mustache and blue eyes. Tall and broad-shouldered, he favored Western boots and ornate belt buckles. He looked, Hilary thought, like something out of Bret Harte, or maybe one of his own paintings.

"Alan get off all right?" Selena asked Hilary.

"Yes."

Selena looked away tracing the pattern of her teaspoon with one fingernail.

"Who's Alan?" questioned Tom.

Was it Hilary's imagination or did the introduction of Alan's name suddenly cast a pall over the party?

"An old friend of Hilary's," Becca answered. "A very handsome Englishman with a penchant for asking questions."

Tom winked at Hilary. "About time Hil had a handsome man asking her questions."

Selena moaned as though in pain and pushed away her plate. "Chauvinism is alive and well in the year 2001."

"Some people need more than almighty Art in their lives, Selena," Tom retorted.

"Some people need more than their wives, apparently."

In the uncomfortable silence that followed, Tom flushed as red as one of his prairie sunsets and said thickly, "If you'll excuse me, *ladies.*"

This was pointedly meant to exclude Selena who flung after Tom's retreating back, "That's right, cowboy, you mosey on home now."

"Selena!" exclaimed Becca, mildly diverted.

Hastily Hilary excused herself, darting after Tom. She caught him just outside the café unlocking the cab to his black pickup.

He climbed into the cab and swore through the open window, "She is such a bitch. God help Serena if she ever does decide to get out on her own."

Meeting Hilary's curious expression he said, "Something you need, Hil?"

"I wanted to ask you if you knew a friend of Bryan's by the name of Alan Xeres?"

"I know him," Tom growled. "What about him?"

"What can you tell me about him?"

"*He's* not the guy you're seeing?"

"No. Why, is he a 'very handsome Englishman?' "

"He's English. I don't know about handsome, although who can figure chicks? Maybe you'd think he was attractive. I think he's a pin-head."

"Why do you say that?"

Tom gestured impatiently. "He's an ass. Talks a big line about who he knows and what he's done, but it's all bullshit. Brags about his big money and stiffs you with the bar tab every time. And his *paintings!*" Tom shuddered.

"That bad? Where do you know him from?"

"He and Kinsale were pals way back when. Wore his welcome out there when he went after Serena. You know how wacko Kinsale is about Serena."

"Yes." Everyone knew how wacko Bryan was about Serena. "What does this Alan look like?"

Tom shrugged. "Tall, rangy. Dark hair. Mustache. Blue eyes, I think. Sounds sorta like me, doesn't he?" He grinned amiably, recovering his usual easy temper.

"Right up to the part about the bar tab," Hilary joked. "We all know you don't touch the stuff."

Tom took a friendly swipe at her and Hilary ducked in choreographed time.

"One last question," she put in as Tom reached forward to turn the key in the ignition. "When was the last time you saw Xeres?"

Tom frowned thinking it over. "Hell, ages ago. Maybe six
months or so. I heard he moved back to England."

***

It was hard to believe how much she missed Alan, Hilary mused
as she climbed the stairs to the loft. She had only known him a few
days. Long enough to understand that Alan was someone it would
take a long time to truly know. All the same, a connection had
formed between them. Hilary did not give her heart lightly; she
believed the caring had been on both sides.

Unless she was turning into one of those batty women who
married men in prison.

For the first time she could remember, Hilary felt lonely. She
let herself into the loft, set down the sack of groceries she had
purchased at the Italian grocers around the corner and pulled out
a newspaper. She smoothed out the smudgy page and stared down
at the photo of Alexander Napier with his colorless cold eyes and
enigmatic smile.

Hilary still felt that Sir Alexander was at the heart of this mystery. She was certain that in the man himself, his character, lay the
answer to Alan's involvement. Dragging a chair over she sat down
backwards in it, shaking out the newspaper folds and reading once
more abut the Smuggler's Bay Murder.

The problem was, she decided a few minutes into scanning
the columns, what she knew about Sir Alexander Napier just didn't
add up. According to the papers Napier had been the thirty-eight
year old *wunderkind* of Scotland Yard. He had been one of their
youngest Chief-Inspectors and was held to be the Yard's foremost
art expert. He had received commendations for bravery and a cita-
tion for performance above and beyond the call of duty, though
under what circumstances was not revealed. As if all this was not
disturbing enough, the man came from a wealthy aristocratic family with a bent towards law enforcement. Napier's father, a Scotland Yard Superintendent, had died in the line of duty. Lord Henry

Archibald, the murdered World War II hero, had been Napier's godfather and mentor at the Yard.

So why did this conservative super-cop suddenly go winging across the Atlantic, setting up secret meets with bad guys, and trying to murder Alan?

"I don't get it," Hilary told Claude. Claude paused in grooming himself to fix her with that blankly intent stare so reminiscent of Alan in certain moods.

"There's a link but where's the motive?"

No matter how she worked it, Hilary could not believe that the Sir Alexander Napier the papers described had turned to a life of crime—not for a million dollars. Not for all the money in the world.

"It's too bad too," she muttered, turning the page, "because other than being dead, he's the perfect suspect."

Reluctantly Hilary had to admit that Alan was right. From the look of things, Napier had been in the States crime-busting. His methods might not comply with the Yard's police manual (or anyone's), but clearly Sir Alexander had believed himself to be on the side of the angels.

Well, now he is for keeps, Hilary thought wryly, studying Napier's Mona Lisa twitch of a smile. And surely the fact that Napier was dead illustrated the faultlessness of his logic?

Napier had to have believed Alan was Alan Xeres when he jumped him. The only problem with that scenario was that if Napier had been pursuing Alan Xeres in connection with these art robberies and murder then he was bound to know what Xeres looked like. Besides, there was Alan's dream of a scuffle in the interrogation room between himself and Napier. That had to be based on partial memory.

It was too convoluted, Hilary reflected. Like this riddle of a caravan of cars (and suspects) arriving and departing from the house at Smuggler's Bay the day of the murder. There were just too many people involved for the thing to be plausible.

The kind of international art ring they were suppositioning

would have to be a tightly run operation. The fewer the people the lesser the risk—and the greater the profit. Basically there were only three 'skills' needed: a thief, a forger and a dealer. If Alan Xeres was the thief, who was the forger?

Who has the necessary degree of skill besides me? Hilary inquired gloomily of herself.

Tom Campbell had the technical ability, but forgery of Old Masters had as much to do with knowledge of style and the practical considerations of forgery: getting the right materials, baking the thing, etc. Besides, Tom had shown no alarm at the mention of Alan Xeres' name, and wouldn't the forger know who his partners were?

Maybe. Maybe not.

Then again there was Bryan. Bryan was a very good painter and he certainly didn't seem to have many moral qualms. He had the requisite skill and he was a pal (or former pal) of Alan Xeres. But Bry, being ever the serious Artiste, might scorn the notion of copying anyone else's work. Even Rembrandt's. Even for huge profit—which incidentally he showed no signs of possessing.

Would anyone be reckless enough to trust Bryan with that kind of dangerous knowledge? No one who knew him well, surely.

Which didn't leave a large list of suspects. Serena had certainly been acting oddly, but she wasn't a painter. And in any case Hilary thought she had a pretty good idea of what lay behind Serena's erratic behavior.

Becca had described herself as a 'good copyist.' Becca knew Grainger intimately, and Napier had believed the Pauley Galleries were implicated. But Napier had also believed Hilary was implicated. Granted Becca had a Bohemian past—she might even find it a lark to imitate the Old Masters. Thumbing her nose at the stuffed shirts she scorned while profiting from. Would Becca risk her hard won contentment for cold cash?

Someone was risking everything.

Selena, a graphic artist, was capable with line and form. She had admitted she had excellent training—and come to think of it, everything Selena had done, Serena had been part of.

Even Grainger had started out as a painter.

Hilary sighed and ran a hand through her cropped hair. The problem was that when you didn't have all the facts there were too many possibilities. Napier had made one error in logic; perhaps there had been others. His mistakes had proven fatal. Hilary couldn't afford to make the same ones.

***

Alan was not having a good day.

It had started out well enough. Actually it had started out quite well indeed, he reflected with a tired grin. It was how the day had gone after he had dragged himself out of Hilary's bed and away from Hilary's soft, warm body.

Thank God for the instincts that had sent him shinnying down the fire escape in full felon mode. Sure enough, when he'd checked out the front of the warehouse there was PC Perseverance waiting grimly at the mouse-hole.

Actually Alan was rather relieved to see the old boy. Anything less would have meant the sergeant was not running to form and that would have brought up a whole new set of concerns. With the good sergeant tailing Hilary everywhere Alan had one less worry. And as long as Hilary kept her head she'd be fine. They couldn't prove much against her without himself, and Alan had no intention of landing in nick.

Stashing his things behind the trash bin down the alley Alan had cut across the park and found a 7-Eleven store. There he bought a copy of *The Recycler,* a gigantic cup of coffee and a dry pastry which he nearly chipped a tooth on as he sat reading on a park bench under the accusing stare of Alex Napier, plastered on an abandoned newspaper.

The Recycler led Alan to a car for sale. Buying the car was a calculated risk. He couldn't rent one without ID, but he could possibly buy one for the right price and from the right person. The right person turned out to be a weedy chap with bloodshot eyes and that vague air which Alan figured made him unlikely to contact the police even if he should recognize his gullible buyer from the *Steeple Hill Gazette.*

It took a good chunk out of Alan's remaining money to buy the battered yellow Pinto. Before long he was going to have a serious cash flow problem. One more on a list of increasingly pressing problems, Alan thought sardonically, folding his long legs into the car.

By the time Alan had filled his new car with petrol the morning was gone. The hazy afternoon was hot and humid. Alan unpeeled his damp back from the plastic upholstery as he pulled up at the Hall of Records and uncoiled from the hot seat.

This was another necessary risk, walking through the Civic Center complex of court house, library and sheriff sub-station, but instinct told him that this was the last place anyone would look for him.

Inside the air-conditioned Hall of Records Alan straightened his sunglasses and headed straight for the County Assessor's Office, where he went directly to work trying to charm the two rather bored women behind the towering stacks of paper. He knew Hilary would have chuckled at the softening effected by the combination of his smile and accent. In no time at all Alan was pouring through books of plat maps.

It didn't take long to find what he was looking for.

The house at Smuggler's Bay and the five acres of undeveloped land surrounding it were indeed for sale. In fact house and land had been on the market for over a year. The man paying the ruinous taxes on the property was Grainger Pauley.

Bulls-eye.

But a name on a deed wasn't proof. In fact it wasn't anything the local lads didn't already know. He needed evidence. Good, old-fashioned conclusive evidence that would stand up in court. And as gratifying as it was to know he was right, Alan also knew this was the easy part. Getting the hard evidence was going to be the challenge.

Leaving the Assessor's Office, Alan's next stop was the nearest hardware store. He made his purchases and started out towards Smuggler's Bay. Heat shimmered on the winding road and lay like steam over the glittering ocean. It was an uncomfortable drive made more uncomfortable by the return of the grinding ache behind his eyes. It was the glare of the sun, Alan thought. That and the Pinto's tendency to backfire. His headache and the moist heat sapped energy and purpose.

What a bloody country, he told himself, scrubbing his hand across his face. About the most one could say for it was that Hilary lived here.

He was still telling himself this several hours later as he perched precariously on the cliffs above the churning waves at Smuggler's bay.

He had spent the afternoon scouring the pigeonhole caves riddling the cliff face. For his trouble he had nearly brained himself on the low ceiling of a dwarf-sized recess. He had received a face full of sand and pebbles in a mini-landslide. He had rope burns, a ripped pair of Levi's, and assorted cuts and bruise from a slight miscalculation that had sent him crashing down the cliff side and very nearly onto the boulders below. But he had not found any paintings. Cobwebs, bird nests, lizards, ground squirrels, and a few crushed beer cans, but no trace that anyone had ever tried to conceal stolen masterpieces in the cliffs at Smuggler's Bay.

Which shot that theory straight to hell, Alan thought wryly. And he was running out of options fast.

***

At four o'clock Hilary began to think in terms of food, realizing that she had consumed nothing but cappuccino and iced coffee all day. She wasn't particularly hungry as she went over her lists of suspects, motives and miscellaneous information for the nth time.

It was sinking in on Hilary that she did not have the methodical mind needed for detective work. Her own deductions were intuitive, based on her knowledge of her friends and colleagues. Logic was Alan's line, but what did the method matter so long as they both came to the same conclusion? In time to keep each other out of jail.

Alan. Hilary sighed, absently chopping cloves of garlic. Could you love someone whose name you didn't even know? Could you love someone you had only known three days? Maybe that was a dumb question because she had gone to bed with him after a mere three days, and that was about as out of character as she could get.

There were people who loved without ever really knowing the person they loved. You heard it on TV all the time. 'I would never have believed he was capable.' How often did some hapless gullible woman speak those fatal words into a microphone?

I may never see him again. Last night may be all we ever have.

Hilary had managed to live thirty years without committing herself to a man. She had occasionally 'fallen in love,' but these were comfortable, brief relationships that had gone nowhere. Passion had been reserved for her work; commitment for her relationship with God. Now she felt passion and commitment for a man who not only did not seem to share her spiritual beliefs, he was in trouble with the law. A man who bore the mark of Cain.

It did not seem possible, yet Hilary truly believed that all things happened for a reason, and she missed Alan more than she would have believed possible four days ago. She missed the way he said her name. She missed his crooked grin when something humorous caught him off guard. She missed his aggravatingly logical brain and the way he looked in his form-fitting Levi's.

Determinedly Hilary pushed this line of thought aside and turned on the tap filling a pan of water and setting it on the stove burner. But as she peeled shrimp for the paella, she found herself wondering if Alan liked shrimp paella? It was disconcerting. She knew so little about him. The food he liked, the music he listened to, the books he preferred, his faith. Truthfully she didn't know if he was a crook or not—and it wasn't that this wasn't important to her, it was; but Alan seemed to be a good man, worthy of loving, worthy of commitment. Love and commitment could make all the difference to someone who had lost their way.

And Hilary did know that though Alan was tough, he could be tender, and that despite his cool self-containment he was a warm and generous lover.

Lover. Hilary's fingers slipped and a shrimp went flying to the delight of Claude who promptly pounced on it.

Hilary left the rice simmering and went around the loft picking up. Her day seemed to have lost focus. In the bath she gathered damp towels out of the hamper thinking, *This is ridiculous. I'm getting misty over his bath towel?*

Impatiently she stuffed everything into her laundry basket, carrying the load downstairs to the basement.

At five o'clock the shop was still open although there was no sign of Selena or Serena, and no customers wandering through the crowded racks. A glance in the open doorway revealed nothing but silent rows of bright clothes and dust motes floating in the shafts of sunlight streaming through the glass doors.

A noise on the basement stairs caught her attention. Hilary turned to see the back of someone coming up from the basement. Long blonde hair swirled like a veil as the woman rounded the banister, her legs moving like pistons as she raced up the stairs.

"Mary?" Hilary called.

Mary, if it was Mary Campbell, did not stop. The next minute she shot out the shop entrance and was gone.

Hilary stared after her, and then slowly continued down the basement steps. The light was on in the basement casting menacing shadows against the dingy wall. Hilary was reminded of the first night Alan had arrived; the angry voices she had heard behind the workshop doors. Today it was cool and silent as a tomb. The doors to the workshop were closed. Nothing seemed out of place, yet her sense of unease persisted.

Disgusted with herself, Hilary loaded the washer and started it. The machine rumbling into life, startling her, and causing her to cast another nervous glance over her shoulder.

The only thing out of place was in the pyramid of large cardboard boxes stacked at the other end of the room. One container seemed to have tumbled off the pile. It lay on its side, turned away from Hilary.

Reluctantly, her sense of dread increasing with each step, Hilary walked towards the box. It appeared as though something heavy stored inside had been tipped half out. She spied a glimpsed of blue and white checked cloth.

Tentatively Hilary tried to lift the box off, but whatever was inside was now weighting down the flaps. She had to use her strength to lever the box forward and dump out its contents.

What came sliding out to sprawl awkwardly on the cement had Hilary catching her breath in horror.

A man's body lay slumped at her feet. Hilary could see every inch of him in precise, minute detail: the long, rag-doll body in its grubby jeans, the ghastly white-blue pallor of the face with a horror of bulging eyes and thrusting tongue. Lank red strands of hair were caught beneath the gleam of wire biting into the narrow throat.

"Oh Lord," whispered Hilary. "*Bryan—*"

CHAPTER ELEVEN

The sideshow of violent death was in full swing.

Black and whites blocked the sidewalk in front of the warehouse, red and blue lights flashing as deputy sheriffs held the crowd of spectators back. A little something special for the Japanese tourists.

In the basement of the warehouse the county coroner was chatting with a gum-chewing forensics expert while the earthly remains of Bryan Kinsale were zipped into a black body bag.

Fingerprints had been dusted, scene of crime photos snapped, and another deputy from the sheriff's department was taping off the head of the basement stairs with yellow ribbon reading: **PO-LICE LINE DO NOT CROSS.** Upstairs Hilary was answering yet another round of questions from Sheriff Huntsinger.

"Now, Miss Jackson, you say that the last time you saw Bryan Kinsale alive was around eleven o'clock last night?"

"Yes."

"You say that you visited Kinsale with a friend, Alan Allen, who has since returned to Great Britain?"

"That's right." How long, Hilary wondered, before the sheriff's department verified that no one named Alan Allen had left this country—or even entered it?

One evasion led to a lie and on to a bigger lie. Was it perjury at this stage or just obstructing justice?

"And you say that you talked about art and that Kinsale asked you to intercede with Grainger Pauley of the Pauley Galleries on his behalf?"

"Yes."

Sheriff Huntsinger had a pair of the chilliest blue eyes Hilary had ever seen. They zeroed on her for a long moment before the sheriff said mildly, "You were especially good friends with Kinsale?"

"Not especially." That sounded heartless. Hilary qualified, "We were friendly. It's a close community."

Taking notes to the side was a trim, blonde assistant-sheriff. Her gaze, briefly meeting Hilary's, was impersonal.

"And did you?"

"Did I? Oh, intercede? I spoke to Grainger about Bryan this morning and he said he had already reconsidered his decision to handle Bryan's work. He was meeting him for a business lunch at one o'clock."

"You went to see Mr. Pauley solely to speak on Bryan Kinsale's behalf?"

"No. Well, that is, Grainger acts as my rep too. I have a show in New York next month. We discussed that."

Hilary wondered how long before Grainger spilled the beans about why she had really been to see him.

Surely the sheriff's department knew everything Sergeant Hogsworth had learned if the sergeant was working with them? But then why wasn't the sergeant with Huntsinger now? Was he following his own leads? According to the *Steeple Hill Gazette* Hogsworth was working in conjunction with the sheriffs; Hilary was not sure why she questioned this.

"Let's get back to the woman you saw leaving here," Sheriff Huntsinger said briskly. "That was at what time?"

"Five. Maybe five-thirty. I wasn't paying attention."

Unconsciously the sheriff stroked his upper lip. "But it was definitely as late as five?"

"I heard the steeple chimes. A few minutes later I came downstairs."

"Tell me once more what you saw."

They had been over this twice already.

"It was very quiet, no one was around, which seemed unusual. The shop closes at six so there are often people still here. Anyway, as I was passing the shop doors I saw a woman coming up the basement steps. She was already turning the corner so I only saw her from behind."

"But you recognized her?"

Hilary shrugged uncomfortably. "I thought so."

"You thought it was Mrs. Mary Campbell, didn't you? Miss Selena Thomas reports she heard you call out, 'Mary.'"

"I wasn't sure."

"That so? So then what did you do?"

"I carried my laundry downstairs and put it in the washer. I felt . . . uneasy. As though I was being watched. I kept looking around, trying to see if anything was out of place. I noticed that some cardboard boxes in the back had been knocked over and I went to check . . ." Hilary swallowed hard, sickness returning at the memory of what she had found.

"These cardboard boxes are generally used for what?" The sheriff changed direction abruptly.

"T-shirts, clothes. Two Deux is a boutique. They handle cloth-ing, jewelry, some gift items. The Thomases silk-screen their own designs here. We clear the basement out every few months but boxes tend to accumulate."

"After you found Bryan Kinsale's body, how long was it before you phoned 911?"

Hilary thought it was no accident the way Huntsinger kept jumping around. He was trying to shake her, see if her story changed at all. Where had she read that the person who discovered a body was considered a prime suspect?

"A couple of minutes. There wasn't any doubt that he was dead. I ran upstairs and Serena was there. We called from the shop."

Into Hilary's mind came that startling first sight of Serena, red-eyed, puffy and pale from crying. "You got here right away."

Hilary remembered those awful minutes waiting with Serena for the police to arrive. She didn't think she and Serena had ex-changed a word after the initial horrified exclamations. They had just sat waiting. Without warning Serena had burst into harsh sobs. Sobs that had nothing to do with grief for Bryan, Hilary knew instinctively as she went to comfort Serena. How strange it was to wait there with Serena who of all people was the person Bryan loved best. Bryan would have been flattered by the tears.

"Were there any hard feelings between the deceased and Mary Campbell?"

"None."

"You didn't pick anything up last night?"

"No."

"What was the nature of the relationship between Mary Campbell and Bryan Kinsale?"

"Mary models for a lot of us. Bryan used her most."

"Would you say they were friends?"

"Yes."

"More than friends?"

"No." Hilary wanted to make the sheriff understand this. "In a way both Mary and Bryan felt like outsiders. It made them allies."

"Outsiders? Why's that?"

"Mary isn't an artist herself. A model doesn't have the same— er—clout with some people in this community. Bryan—Bryan could be difficult."

"Someone sure thought so. How do you mean difficult?"

"Out of sync with the rest of—" She nearly said 'us' and was disgusted with herself.

"He had enemies?"

"That's too strong a word. He—"

Huntsinger smiled a cold sort of smile. "Kinsale had enemies, Ms Jackson. No one accidentally garrotes himself. Is there anything you'd like to add to this statement?"

"No."

Huntsinger rose abruptly. "All right then. Call us if you think of anything, Ms. Jackson. No matter how trivial you think it is. Murder gets to be a habit real quick."

Hilary was startled. That had been too easy. Not a mention of Alan Xeres or Scotland Yard inspectors or stolen art.

"That's it? You're leaving?"

"We'll be in touch," the sheriff said laconically.

Long after the sheriff had gone and the sounds of official activity downstairs ceased, Hilary continued to stare at the newsprint photo of Sir Alexander Napier.

"It's your fault really," she told the photograph.

Napier of course had no answer but that infuriating smile. Hilary sighed, starting to push the paper away. But something about the photo caught her attention. There was something curiously familiar about it. Was it simply because she had seen it before?

Frowning she tried to look past the cavalier-style mustache and beard to study the shape of those pale, ironic eyes, the forehead where the hair sprang in a dark widow's peak.

The idea that presented itself was so wild that Hilary instantly dismissed it. And yet . . .

So much of what she had taken for granted was based on other people's information. Who was to say that all that information was correct? Other people's information could be colored by opinions and assumptions—even their own motives. Perhaps she had accepted unquestioningly as fact what was actually someone's deliberate fiction.

Hilary reached for the phone then stopped. Serena and Selena had both been through a lot today. The disadvantage of catching people off-balance was that sometimes they pulled you over the edge with them.

***

It was midnight.

The only light visible from his vantage point was the light in Hilary's loft. Once in a while he caught a glimpse of the top of her dark head. Apparently Hilary was pacing the floor. A most un-Hilary-like behavior.

The sound of music reached him faintly. It sounded Middle Eastern and mysterious. Loreena McKennitt? He had not figured

Hilary for a New Ager, but then there was a world of things he didn't know about the woman.

As he listened, tired and cold in the damp night air, the haunting music seemed to emphasize his isolation, his loneliness. The tight check he had held on himself all day was beginning to give way. He wanted to see her, to reassure himself that she really was all right.

He felt to blame for bringing this new disaster upon her. He should have kept closer watch. He should have anticipated this. Their amateurish poking around was stirring someone up. Sheer luck that someone had gone after Kinsale and not Hilary. Was that because Kinsale was involved and had lost his nerve? Or because Kinsale held some piece of information he had not revealed to Hilary and Alan last night? Had something enabled Kinsale to add two and two together? Did someone consider Kinsale a weak link and therefore expendable? Or was Kinsale an interested bystander just stupid enough to try a spot of blackmail? Alan had not foreseen Kinsale's death and it worried him. What else was he missing?

Next time they might come after Hilary. He should have considered this before. Panic was making someone dangerous. He had to make Hilary understand this. If he could get her to go away for a time, so much the better.

The sheriff's menagerie had finally cleared out. Odds on that someone had been left to keep an eye on the place, but so far he had been unable to spot anyone. Except for the far-off music it was quiet. Too quiet? The shadows around the building deepened, lengthened like fingers reaching out. He shook off that bit of fancy and soundlessly moved another foot forward.

Still nothing.

He had to damp down his impatience. She was all right. He could see she was all right. No one was holding a gun or knife on her. But he had been dogged all day by this increasing sense of urgency—almost anxiety. Knowing was not proof. And every hour brought the walls closing in on him—and Hilary with him.

Pressure built up behind his eyes, bringing back one of the throbbing headaches that had plagued him since his accident. He compartmentalized the pain as he had learned to compartmentalize so many things in his life.

He could just make out the outline of the fire escape dully gleaming in the light from above. Climbing it was bound to create a hell of a racket, but the front and rear exits were most likely to be under surveillance.

Rising stiffly, Alan covered the last feet of ground between himself and his target, swinging himself up on the fire escape. As anticipated there was a screech of metal rungs that raised the hair on the back of his neck.

A bulky shadow detached itself from the alley fence and launched itself at Alan's long figure as he dangled from the fire escape.

Alan's grip was torn from the steel rungs as he was tackled about the waist. He slammed back into the wall, the back of his head hit brick, and for an instant he saw stars. His hands went slack as the neon flashes filled his vision.

"Gotcha!" the deep, familiar voice of Detective-sergeant Hogsworth exclaimed triumphantly.

The street stopped whirling. Alan's gaze cleared. He began to struggle, bucking like mad, twisting frantically in those bear-like arms. No joy. He brought his knee up in his aggressor's groin. Hogsworth grunted and swore, his grasp shifting momentarily.

That move should have done for him, but he was a tough old bird, this Scotland Yard sergeant. He knew a trick or two himself.

"Oh no you don't," he gasped, and somehow his arm was clamping down on Alan's throat in a chokehold.

Alan's fingers clawed at the vise-like band cutting off his oxygen. It was like trying to shift a tree trunk. Alan continued to wrestle, wriggling like a manic contortionist. His senses swam. With his remaining strength he jabbed his elbow into Hogsworth's gut.

Hogsworth's breath expelled on a long *umphh*. He released Alan in surprise.

Hungrily Alan sucked air into his burning lungs. He didn't want to cripple the old boy but things were more desperate than anticipated. As Hogsworth made another dive, Alan swung a right with all his might. The shock of that impact shivered all down his arm.

Hogsworth staggered back into a collection of trash bins with a mighty clanging. Alan ran, leaping for the tall wooden fence with less than his usual agility. His hands closed over the top and he dragged himself up, balancing precariously for half a moment on the fence.

The white circle of a spotlight beam caught him squarely. Alan's eyes squinted against the blinding glare.

"*Sir Alex!*" Sergeant Hogsworth exclaimed in stupefied accents. "My God, man, I thought you were *dead!*"

The words rippled through Alex like a jolt of electricity. He felt the floodgates of memory give way with a splintering sound that tore through his brain. A tidal wave of remembrance rushed in sweeping everything along in its black, boiling wake.

His hands let go of the wooden fence and he plunged down into the darkness . . .

***

Hilary was already awake when the pounding began on her front door. It was fortunate that she had showered and dressed because she got the feeling the sheriff deputies would have insisted she accompany them to the station in chenille bathrobe and mules rather than waste any time changing clothes.

In no time at all she was sitting in a windowless room across from Sheriff Huntsinger. The blonde assistant sheriff sat in the corner. There was a cassette recorder on the table between them taking down every word Hilary said.

"Let's go back to the night of the fifth, Ms Jackson. The night you and Alan Allen paid a visit to Bryan Kinsale. Did Kinsale say or do anything that evening to indicate he was afraid for his life?"

"Of course not."

"Did he indicate he was having problems with someone? A dispute over money perhaps?"

"Bryan was always short of money. I don't recall any disputes over it."

"Did he owe you money?"

"No. Anything I gave Bryan I considered a gift."

"Pretty generous. Kinsale get along well with everyone?"

Hilary opened her mouth, met the sheriff's calculating gaze and fell silent. Huntsinger had done his background checks. He knew exactly how Bryan's colleagues felt about him.

Huntsinger did not pursue this line. Instead he questioned, "How well do you know Alan Allen, Miss Jackson?"

This was it. Hilary swallowed. She couldn't help glancing at the red light on the tape recorder. "I—uh, I know he couldn't have had anything to do with Bryan's death."

"Because he has returned to England?"

Hilary stared mutely.

"You are good friends, you and Allen?"

"Yes."

"Lovers?"

"I don't see—"

"Partners?"

"In what?"

"You tell me."

"Tell you what?"

Huntsinger tossed a navy passport book and a leather wallet with several pieces of official ID on the scratched table top. "This may save time."

Hilary reached out to pick up the driver's license noting absently that her fingers were trembling slightly. She stared at the photo.

"This is the man you know as Alan Allen?"

She nodded, unable to find her voice.

The information was all there on these pieces of laminated

plastic. Alexander Jamieson Napier, age 38, height 6'1", weight 170, hair black, eyes green. Citizen of the United Kingdom, birthplace Edinburgh, Scotland. Another square of officialese proclaimed Alexander Jamieson Napier a Detective Chief-Inspector with the Metropolitan Police, Criminal Investigation Department, Art Thefts Division.

There were credit cards and a membership to a men's club. No personal effects such as letters or photos, just a neat array of facts and figures which tallied with a picture of a man who led an orderly, focused, completely self-contained existence.

"You don't seem as surprised as I'd have expected, Ms Jackson."

"I—I had guessed at something like this," Hilary managed. "But it seemed so—it seemed impossible that you—that the police would have made such a mistake."

Huntsinger said grimly, "Mistakes happen." Hilary could see that this particular mistake was something he took a dark view of. "Especially when vital information is withheld from us. Not that we wouldn't have known the truth by this morning when the fingerprint results arrived from Scotland Yard."

Hilary wondered at the deliberate false identification of Napier's body by Sergeant Hogsworth. What had the man hoped to gain for either of them?

"Where is Alan?"

"Napier is at St. Justin's," the sheriff replied shortly. "His sergeant brought him into the emergency room at about one o'clock this morning."

"Is he all right?" Hilary couldn't help the anxiety her voice revealed. Her hands clasped each other in unconscious prayer as she waited tensely for the answer.

Huntsinger picked up Alex's passport and wallet. It seemed to Hilary that he was avoiding her eyes. "They're running tests," he said evasively.

Running tests? What did that mean? What kind of tests? Why had Alan been brought to an emergency room? What had happened to reunite him with Hogsworth? Had someone tried to kill him too?

"Now, Ms. Jackson, tell me about last Friday evening when you first met Sir Alexander Napier." He rolled the syllables of Alan's name as though they were physically painful to him.

Surely there was nothing to be helped by lying any longer? Alan had his own identity back. The police could see that he was one of the good guys. Even if he had not regained his memory it was pretty easy to follow Alan's footsteps since arriving in the States. Easy to see he had been chasing crooks however unorthodox his methods. And in any case her lies wouldn't hold water ten minutes. Not with Huntsinger, who probably knew more than she did at this point.

As accurately as possible Hilary recounted her first meeting with Alan and most of what had subsequently happened. At certain points in her narrative she could see Sheriff Huntsinger exchanging looks with his assistant. That look convinced Hilary that she was right in not confiding in Huntsinger about the trip to Alan Xeres' home, or about breaking into Napier—Alan's actually—hotel room at the Seven Palms.

She was pretty sure Hogsworth would not reveal anything that might damn his chief in the local authorities' eyes.

When Hilary had completed her statement the sheriff removed the cassette from the tape recorder. He and his assistant excused themselves leaving Hilary to her thoughts in the depressing little room.

Minutes dragged by. One long minute after another until twenty minutes had passed by her wristwatch.

Finally the sheriff and his assistant returned with a typed statement which Hilary was asked to sign. Hilary signed the triplicate forms and handed the sheaf of papers back to the sheriff expecting an end to the interrogation.

"Who—" her voice cracked with dryness. Hilary swallowed and tried again. "Whose body was it at Smuggler's Bay if it wasn't Al—Napier's?"

"Another British national. A small time thief and ex-con by the name of Alan Xeres. Ever hear of him?"

"The name is familiar."

"I bet." The sheriff smiled a smile that made Hilary uneasy. He scanned the typed sheets of her statement.

"Now, Ms. Jackson," he said, still staring at the papers, "in your statement you say Napier appeared dazed and confused. Did neither of you consider contacting the authorities? The sheriff's department? The paramedics?"

With a sinking sensation Hilary realized the interrogation was far from over. In fact, armed with her statement, they were now about to enter upon a second phase of trying to trip her up.

"Alan—Alex was convinced he wasn't badly hurt. He felt that if he could lie down for an hour or two his memory would return."

"I see. And when his memory did not return?"

Hilary stared. What could she answer? That Alan was afraid to go to the police? That Alan himself believed he had murdered Xeres, or at least planned to murder him in cold blood? She raised her chin. "Are you charging me with something, Sheriff?"

Huntsinger, momentarily taken aback, recovered fast.

"Why no, Ms. Jackson," he said evenly. "We're simply trying to put together the pieces of what happened. From the doctor's diagnosis Napier seems to have been suffering from some kind of post-traumatic shock. We're just curious as to why a police officer in trouble would avoid going to the police for help. You'd think it would be his first instinct."

"Probably because it was ingrained in his subconscious that he was trying to go around the local police. Trying to dodge red tape, I mean, not because he planned to murder anybody."

"Yep, he strikes me as a loose cannon too," the sheriff agreed.

Hilary decided this man had a small-town chip on his shoulder and a mind already set in stone.

"That's not what I mean. I know Alex well enough to know that he would have tried to strike a deal with Xeres to get him to reveal who was behind these art thefts. He wouldn't kill his only lead to the person ultimately responsible for Lord Henry's death."

"Maybe he already knew who that was," Huntsinger pointed

out. "I bet he knows now. And I bet he's not telling us for the same reason he didn't come to us about Xeres."

The implication was clear: vengeance. A personal vendetta. And Hilary had probably just filled in the blanks for whatever case they were trying to build against Alan.

She said quietly, "If you're not charging me, I'd like to leave now. I've told you everything I know."

"I doubt that, Ms Jackson."

Now she understand why she had been dragged down to the station. So that they could intimidate her, scare her into betraying Alan.

The sheriff smiled. "We do have a few more questions."

"Then I'd like to have my attorney present."

Sheriff Huntsinger lowered the papers he held. "That's a funny request for an innocent citizen to make."

"Is it?"

"Yes it is, Ms. Jackson. Generally people who have nothing to hide don't start screaming for their lawyers right off the bat."

Hilary checked her wristwatch. "I don't think two and a half hours is 'right off the bat.' Frankly, Sheriff, I think you're hoping I'm going to somehow incriminate myself."

"You feel that's a possibility?"

Hilary met his eyes steadily. The Sheriff shrugged.

"I'm not interested in putting a talented young lady like yourself in jail, Ms Jackson. I'm interested in Napier. You two got pretty close this weekend, didn't you?"

Hilary said, hoping she sounded calmer than she felt, "I think your last comment explains why I need legal council."

The sheriff sat back in his chair and tossed her statement aside. "Suit yourself. Just make sure whose side you want to be on, Ms. Jackson. Once someone crosses that final line of killing someone else; well, the killing just keeps getting easier."

CHAPTER TWELVE

"I am sorry, sir," Sergeant Hogsworth apologized. "I should have realized you had the situation well in hand."

It was as well the man at the window had his back to his sergeant. His expression was a study.

"I don't follow why you allowed the sheriff's department to think I was dead," Sir Alexander Napier questioned, turning from his view of the hospital parking lot.

They were in a small private room at St. Justin's. All morning long doctors had run various tests on Alex: from x-rays to brain scans. They were currently trying to convince him of the merits of something called cerebral angiography which sounded bloody awful and which Alex steadfastly refused.

Hogsworth belatedly filled the Yanks in on a few minor points he had neglected to mention during his original briefings with Huntsinger. He had worn out his lukewarm welcome; this visit to his super's room was unsanctioned to say the least. But Hogsworth, cradling his pipe and watching Alex prowl the small bare room, was unperturbed. It took a great deal to perturb Hogsworth. Only recently had he discovered how much.

"It's this way, Sir Alex: initially I suppose I hoped you might be playing out your own hand. I didn't want to risk interfering." His stolid face tightened. "Later when I believed you were dead, I hoped to keep the perpetrator off-guard by confusing the issue."

Alex's crooked grin flickered. "What you mean is you had no intention of leaving Mr. Pauley to the tender mercies of our cousins across the water."

"That may have been a consideration," conceded Hogsworth

comfortably. "I understand extradition papers are in the works at Headquarters."

"We haven't a hope of extraditing Pauley without some kind of evidence."

"Have to get the evidence, I suppose." Hogsworth didn't sound concerned. But then Hogsworth had always had an unnerving faith in the infallibility of the chief he had helped train.

"Easier said than done. Tell me this, Sam, how did I happen to be wrongfully identified in the first place?"

Hogsworth's granite features almost cracked into a smile. "The only ID on Xeres was your own. Your passport, your billfold, even your watch and signet ring—the buggering little thief. And as you're of similar age and appearance, same height and build, dark hair and light eyes, why I suppose it was a natural enough mistake. Don't know why no one noticed that Xeres's eyes were blue not green," Hogsworth added severely. "That was sheer carelessness."

"But surely . . .?"

"The clincher was that cab driver ID-ing Xeres as the man he drove to Smuggler's Bay. You see, sir, you were both wearing blue jeans and white shirts and you looked superficially enough alike that the cabby assumed you were his fare. Not an observant chap." Hogsworth added, "As you've often remarked, most people aren't— observant that is. Now if I hadn't come along and positively iden- tified you, why I suppose someone would have smelled a rat before the Yard matched your prints as the unidentified set found at the crime scene. It slowed things considerably submitting the wrong prints to the wrong departments."

"Stranger things have happened, I suppose," Alex muttered, "although I can't think of any off hand." He thrust his hands in the pockets of his battered Levi's and inquired, "How much did you have to give John Wayne?"

Hogsworth grunted and drew on his pipe. "I hadn't a hell of a lot maneuvering room, sir. They had the Jackson woman in first thing this morning and apparently she decided to make a clean breast of *your* involvement."

Alex did not comment on his sergeant's sarcastic tone. It was not going to be easy explaining Hilary.

"The sheriff's a canny man but I didn't like the noises he was making last night."

"Such as?"

Hogsworth looked uncharacteristically uncomfortable. "No imagination, these bloomin' cowboys. They've been telexing Headquarters all day."

"Building their case?" suggested Alex who deciphered this to mean that the sheriff's department was less than satisfied with his involvement in the case. "What have they got on Hil—on Ms Jackson?"

"Nothing until yesterday when Kinsale was found in her cellar."

"Hardly *her* cellar," Alex objected mildly.

"That posed a bit of a puzzler for me, sir," confessed Hogsworth. "You were so sure when you left home that she was in this thing up to her baby blues. I daresay that's one reason it never occurred that you were the mysterious bloke staying with her."

Alex opened his mouth but was forestalled by a peremptory knock on the door. The door swung open and a lean scarecrow of a man about fifty wearing a khaki sheriff's uniform and insignia strode into the room followed by a young female assistant.

Sheriff Huntsinger's blue eyes lighted on Detective-sergeant Hogsworth. An expression of ire crossed his face.

"What are you doing here? Who let you in? I gave orders he wasn't to be disturbed."

"I was not aware of such orders," Hogsworth returned woodenly. "In any case may I remind you, Sheriff Huntsinger, that Sir Alexander is a British—"

"That's all right, Sergeant," Alex cut in. The last thing they needed to do was antagonize this man. To take down Pauley and his associates they would need all the help they could get. "Would you let Superintendent Mahoney know I'll be faxing a full report this afternoon?"

"Very good sir." Sergeant Hogsworth departed, his expression indecipherable.

Sheriff Huntsinger seemed unimpressed by this display of efficiency. And with good reason, Alex thought wryly. Alex took a seat by the window, crossing his long legs at the ankles with an appearance of ease he did not feel.

"Feel up to answering a few questions?" the sheriff asked, his smile not reaching his eyes.

"Certainly."

"Memory recovered? Didn't forget the past couple of days after you remembered everything previous to getting conked on the head, did you?"

"No. There are a couple of blanks however."

"Somehow I figured you'd say that." Huntsinger took the chair facing Alex's. The assistant sheriff wandered casually over towards the closet. Too late, Alex could have told her. If there had been anything incriminating on him last night Hogsworth would have it by now. No one thinks more like a crook than a cop.

"Why don't we start with what you do remember once you got off the plane in San Francisco?"

"Sure." Alex's eyes flicked to the assistant sheriff.

Huntsinger watched Alex watching his assistant and said laconically, "Chavez will just take down your statement. That is unless you'd prefer to wait for legal council?"

Alex felt as though he had woken up in a minefield. He replied coolly, "That won't be necessary."

"Good. Let's take it nice and slow. You got off the plane in Frisco . . ."

Forty-five minutes later they were still taking it nice and slow and Alex could feel a trickle of perspiration between his shoulder blades. *Never let them see you sweat,* he warned himself.

"You see my dilemma, don't you, Alex? Okay if I call you Alex?"

"Why not?"

The sheriff smiled grimly. "I'm a simple man. Just your average everyday hick cop, and I don't know a genuine Rembrandt from a Rorschach. You're rambling about international art scams and murder plots, but the only thing I see clearly is *you* had motive and you had opportunity. Hell, one of the few points you're clear on is you *did* kill Xeres, although you claim self-defense. Now the autopsy confirms that Xeres had, to cut the technical jargon, a thin patch in his skull. So it wouldn't take much of a blow to kill him. His dying as he did was a freak accident. Maybe even poetic justice if you go for that pap."

Alex wasn't buying the hick cop routine. He knew exactly where Huntsinger was going with this, and the man's blind logic made his blood run cold.

"The part that sticks in my craw," Sheriff Huntsinger informed him, "Is that you came over here hunting Xeres. You knew damn well he'd killed the man who was like a second father to you but you hadn't been able to nail him for it. I feel for you. I do. You saw him getting away; so you hopped a plane without a word to your own department or even your own sergeant. You cashed in your vacation time and off you went into the friendly skies. But once you got here you didn't follow any proper channels I'm familiar with. You sure as hell didn't contact us to enlist our aid. You didn't even stop by to say howdy. Nope, you set up a private meet with Xeres in an abandoned house. That in my mind would add up to a case of premed except for the accident of Xeres having a glass skull. As it is, it looks like second degree homicide."

"I see. Then I'm under arrest?"

His lack of emotion clearly annoyed the sheriff.

"Not yet you're not," he barked. "For one thing you're in the hospital having tests. For another, there are a couple of points in your favor, and as much as I'd like to slam the door on you and throw away the key I can't close my eyes to facts. For one thing Xeres apparently planned on offing you too—and he was a mite more efficient about it. He was carrying a.38 special, which we've traced to him. He also had your wallet, passport and personal effects. I don't think you're shrewd enough to have planted them."

"Thanks," Alan murmured.

"I think the plan was to kill you and dump your body in the ocean and let time and tide do the rest. But either Xeres was too greedy to chuck a gold watch and the other stuff to the fish or he got a kick out of taking your personal effects. You two had history so I'd guess."

Yes, Alex thought dourly, it would have given Xeres a rush to lift Alex's belongings, and he was just stupid enough and arrogant enough to flaunt his possession of them.

"Furthermore we have the doc's report that Xeres nearly brained you with the butt of his own gun. We have this medical anomaly of the paper-thin patch on Xeres' skull, which you couldn't have known about. We have the results of your tests so it's unlikely you were faking the amnesia. I was here when your sergeant brought you in last night and you looked half-dead to me."

"Too kind."

"Last but not least," Huntsinger snapped, "we know that Xeres had to have suggested the meeting place. You hadn't been here twenty-four hours. We have the fact that you made no effort to conceal your identity coming over here, and the fact that you weren't carrying a piece."

"I do see your dilemma," Alex commented. "You can't quite make the old necktie fit and you're too good a cop to adjust the size."

"You are an arrogant bastard," Huntsinger growled. "If it was up to me . . . I don't like to see a brother cop take the fall for a slime-ball like Xeres, even if that cop is a smart-ass hot-shot Chief-Inspector from Scotland Yard with fifty-dollar shirts and the kind of fancy title we fought a revolution to get rid of."

The sheriff paused for breath and Chavez peeked a quick admiring glance at him.

"But it ain't up to just me," Huntsinger continued darkly. "I got to answer to people. And there's this little matter of this Bryan Kinsale turning up garroted in the house you were staying in."

"What possible motive would I have for killing Kinsale? You couldn't possibly make that stick."

"You have an alibi?"

Alex laughed wryly.

"Well then we'll have to see about that, won't we?"

"Then I'm under arrest?"

The sheriff pressed his lips together tightly. "I haven't made my mind up. I will ask you not to leave town or even this hospital room without my authorization."

Alex's nod was curt.

The sheriff rose and lumbered out followed by his assistant. Before the door closed behind them Alex heard her murmur, "Cool customer."

***

"It's police harassment, my pet," Grainger was telling Hilary for the third time as she stood, cradling the phone, gazing out at the green field of ocean. Celadon was the name of that particular shade, the translucent, mysterious green glaze used in 12th Century sung Dynasty ceramics. Did Alan—Alex—know his eyes were celadon-green?

"We've got to get you out of here," Grainger's tinny voice urged.

"Grainger, the sheriffs aren't going to let me go anywhere. Where would I go?"

"To New York. To see about the new show."

"I'm a material witness, whatever that means."

"What nonsense! You stumbled over a body. It could happen to anyone. My lawyer will arrange everything."

Hilary attempted to quell her rising impatience. "It's more than my finding Bry. It's my association with Alex Napier."

"I don't want to say I told you so . . ." In the face of Hilary's silence Grainger changed tack. "They can't build a case on that. You were simply being a—a Good Samaritan, and he dragged you into this mess. You have to tell them the truth that's all."

"I have told them the truth. Why are you in such a hurry to get rid of me?"

Hilary intended that only half-seriously but the pause that followed sounded sharp and offended.

"What a thing to say," Grainger said finally. "I'm not trying to 'get rid of you,' as you so melodramatically put it. I'm thinking of the show and our reputation. The reputation of the gallery. Murder isn't exactly good for business."

"It won't do any harm in Bryan's case though, will it?"

"*What?*" Grainger sounded stunned. Why he should bother dissembling over such a patent truth Hilary couldn't imagine. Of course Bryan's death would increase the value of his paintings. Death increased the value of any artist's work.

Unfortunately it also put an end to their productivity.

"I'm not saying whatever it is you think I'm saying, Grainger," Hilary told him carefully.

"What is it you think I think you're saying?"

Hilary gave an uneasy laugh. "This conversation isn't making any sense." It was a new experience to have to be so careful with Grainger. He was touchy all at once. Defensive. "I simply meant— look, it wasn't in very good taste, whatever I meant."

"No it wasn't."

"I apologize." For what am I apologizing, she wondered? Is everyone losing it or just me? "Back to what we were originally discussing, which is that the sheriff is not going to let me go. They will probably arrest me."

"Arrest *you?* For what?"

"For aiding and abetting Alex Napier."

"Then they have arrested him?" The note in Grainger's voice could have signaled dismay or delight.

"I got the impression the only reason they hadn't so far was because he's still under doctor's care."

"I see." Impossible to read anything from that. "You pack your duds, my pet. I'll take care of the rest of it."

"But Grainger—"

Hilary's protest was cut off by the decisive click on the other end of the line.

***

The afternoon lagged.

Left to his own devices Alex found himself wearing a hole in the institutional-blue carpet of his hospital room. He knew Huntsinger was playing a waiting game with him—and winning. That was inevitable given the time factor Alex knew he was working against. As galling as it was, he had to play this by Huntsinger's rules.

After lunch he asked to see the sheriff again. Hours passed. Alex knew that too was deliberate. He had let enough suspects cool their heels in his own time.

The sheriff's department wasn't repeating their mistake of the morning, and Alex had no visitors. No communication with Hogsworth. No news on what was happening outside this room. No word of Hilary.

Around tea time—or what would be tea time in a civilized country—Huntsinger finally showed. He had apparently spent a satisfying day barking up the wrong tree. He exuded smug confidence at Alex's summons.

"Well, Alex, what can I do for you?"

"I have a proposition of sorts."

"A proposition? For me? Sure, shoot." Huntsinger beckoned magnanimously with one callused hand.

"Give me forty-eight hours before you charge either myself or Miss Jackson and I'll deliver proof as to who killed Bryan Kinsale."

The proposition Huntsinger anticipated had been something more in the nature of plea-bargaining. Napier's challenge threw him off-balance for a minute. Absently he smoothed the top of his bare lip.

"What about Alan Xeres?"

"You know bloody well that was self-defense."

"Yeah? I think a jury might look at the way you dogged him over here and think you might have had some responsibility in it."

With difficulty Alex reined in his temper. Anger was a luxury he couldn't afford. Huntsinger was less than hours from charging him formally. And even though they both knew with two police departments, a Consulate and everyone's grandmother involved Huntsinger would eventually have to settle for involuntary manslaughter, the damage would be done. Valuable time would be lost. Evidence would be lost. Alex might never be able to prove his case against Pauley and Pauley's surviving accomplice.

Furthermore it wasn't going to do his career much good getting charged with murder in any degree. He was already on thin ice with the brass following the fiasco which had resulted in Lord Henry's murder.

As for what arrest would mean to Hilary . . . He pushed the thought away and said flatly, "I'll get you proof of that as well."

The sheriff's brows rose skeptically. "Physical evidence? Something to hold up in court?"

"I'll build you a tighter case than you have against me now."

"Pretty damn sure of yourself, aren't you?"

"Yes."

The sheriff laughed, this time with real amusement. "And all you want is for me to wait forty-eight hours to charge you and the girl?"

"I want you to give me a free hand," Alex said grimly. "No interference. No tail."

"No back-up?"

"My own back-up."

Alex watched Huntsinger weighing it. Yet what did the man have to lose? They would watch him regardless of what Huntsinger promised. Alex would not be catching any planes out of the country. If they gave him enough rope he would either hang himself or solve their case for them; that's what Huntsinger was figuring. It was the way Alex would figure it himself.

"What the hell." Huntsinger shrugged. "But you've got just twenty-four hours."

"It's not enough time."

"Take it or leave it."

Alex didn't have to consider. "Agreed."

After a moment's hesitation Huntsinger offered a massive hand.

After another moment's hesitation Alex shook it.

***

"Is this a bad time?" Hilary stood hesitating in the doorway of the Thomas's apartment.

Selena shrugged and stepped aside. In the late afternoon light she looked tired and drawn. Her ruby lipstick stood out blood-like against the pallor of her skin. Today Selena looked every day of her forty-odd years.

"Sit," she invited with none of her usual warmth.

Hilary folded her leggy length into one of the low chairs and Selena took the companion chair across from her.

"How's Serena doing?"

"Okay. She's lying down. We decided not to open the shop today with all the reporters and sightseers around." She shivered. "Ghouls."

"Bry's death hit her pretty hard. Not that there was much love lost between any of us. Well, maybe that's why. Serena's too soft-hearted."

Hilary made some non-committal murmur. She picked at the threadbare knee of her jeans and said, "We've been friends a long time."

"Ten years." Selena's amber eyes held Hilary's troubled blue-gray gaze. "Since you moved down here from Seattle. You were just a kid then. Remember? Scrubbed and shining and stubborn as hell."

Hilary twitched a smile.

"You were still illustrating books. *My Friend Jesus.*"

"I remember."

"We thought you were crazy. We thought Grainger was crazy." She sighed. "We've had some good times here, the three of us." Restlessly she jumped to her feet and strode into the kitchen.

Hilary watched Selena open the fridge and pour two glasses of sun tea. She gave up beating around the bush.

"Why was Mary here yesterday?"

"Why don't you ask her? The police did."

"I'm asking you."

Selena ignored this, handing Hilary a glass and unhurriedly seating herself. She tucked her legs Yogi-style beneath her.

"You're covering for Serena, aren't you?"

Selena barely flicked her a glance. "Covering what for Serena?"

"Her affair with Tom Campbell."

Selena said nothing.

"That's why Mary was here that day, wasn't it? To confront Serena? Or to find some kind of proof of their relationship."

"Well, I don't think she was strangling Bryan in the laundry room."

"No. Anyway, the timing's all wrong." Hilary rubbed her forehead tiredly. "The sheriff said Bryan had been dead at least a couple of hours by the time the ME arrived. Do you have any idea why Bry would come here after his lunch with Grainger?"

Selena brushed her long mane over her shoulder. "What's with the Jessica Fletcher routine? How do I know why Bryan showed up? I wasn't here myself. Knowing Bryan, he came to see Serena as usual."

"Doesn't that seem a little weird?"

"Bryan was more than a little weird."

"But they weren't getting along lately."

"So? He probably wanted to gloat. To show off. Grainger had finally agreed to handle his work, hadn't he?"

Hilary's eyes wandered about the familiar room with its woven Indian rugs and furniture upholstered in bright primary colors. On the far wall Selena had painted a mural of Paris. Had Selena ever been to Paris? To Notre Dame? Reluctantly Hilary returned to the hunt.

"Serena was upset about something before I ever knocked on your door. She had left the shop unattended to come in here and cry. I think Mary must have gone downstairs to try and find some proof that Tom and Serena were involved. Instead she found Bryan."

"That lets out Mary and my sister. So who does that leave? Me? Sure. But you were here too—and your pal Alan was running loose. Is that what you're after?" Selena sounded amused; her eyes were anything but. She took a sip from her glass.

Hilary refused to be detoured. "Can you think of any reason why someone would kill Bryan?"

"I can think of plenty reasons to *want* to kill Bryan. To actually do it seems extreme. If anyone in Steeple Hill had really wanted to kill Bryan they would have done it years ago. I know you don't want to believe this but I think the police have the right man in custody."

"I don't." Hilary set her glass aside. "I think you're covering up for someone."

"Come on, Hil. Who? You've said yourself Serena couldn't have killed Bryan. There's no one else I'd cover for. Face it, the killer is Alex or whatever his name is. That first night I met him he seemed a little too intense. Too cool and controlled. Maybe getting hit on the head caused temporary insanity. Who knows? All I'm sure of is I didn't kill Bry; I don't think you did, and Serena didn't. Who does that leave?"

Hilary could think of a few people. She had the brains not to name them. She thought how strange it was that you could know someone for ten years and not know them at all. Maybe you never knew anyone unless you were married to them—or were their twin sister.

She rose to leave. "We both know it's not going to end here, Selena."

Selena also stood. "It better, for all of our sakes. Let me tell you something, Hilary, I'm not the only one who will resent being questioned like this. *Let it go.*"

"I can't."

"He can't mean that much to you! You've only known him a few days!"

"It has nothing to do with Alan. Alex. Not really. And I wish I *could* let it go. I wish things could go back to the way they were. But it's too late."

Hilary moved to the door and opened it. Selena's harsh voice stopped her.

"Hilary, you better think about what you're saying, about what you're risking."

She couldn't believe this had happened between herself and Selena. "Are you threatening me?"

"I'm warning you. There's a difference."

"Thanks for the warning."

Hilary stepped out into the dark hallway. Her last glimpse of Selena before the door closed was of a woman whose pale face and fierce eyes revealed fear.

Hilary turned.

Out of the shadows loomed a tall figure. Hilary opened her mouth to scream. Her cry was cut off by the hand that clamped across her mouth as she was dragged away from the doorway.

CHAPTER THIRTEEN

Hilary kicked and flailed as she was hauled towards the stairs. Light from the street entrance fell on her attacker's face. Hilary's eyes went wide. She stopped struggling.

"Alan!" She mouthed against his hand.

Alex released her and Hilary staggered.

"Are you crazy?" she gasped.

"Keep your voice down." Alex glanced towards the Thomas's closed door.

"You scared me to death!"

"I meant to. What the hell are you playing at?"

"I was—I thought you were under arrest. I was trying to help."

"By becoming the next victim? Rather a drastic means of providing an alibi, don't you think?"

Despite the acerbic tone he did not seem really angry. In fact he seemed a little amused even. She couldn't quite take it in that it really was Alex standing there smirking at her.

"What are you doing skulking around here? I thought they had you under armed guard in the hospital."

"I'm on parole."

"Are you all right? What happened to you?"

"I'm fine."

He looked fine. He looked better than fine in Levi's and a green chambray workshirt. Those pale green eyes watched the movement of her mouth as intently as though he were lip-reading.

Before Hilary could form the next question he had pulled her back into his arms. His mouth fastened on hers, warm and familiar. All Hilary's doubts, fears, angers melted away like honey in the sun. But before she could really relax and enjoy herself Alex dug his fingers into her shoulders and glared at her.

"Make up your mind," snapped Hilary. "Are you going to kiss me or yell at me?"

"Neither. Both. I could strangle you myself. Why are you poking around like some girl detective in a novel? These people are killers."

An uneasy clearing of throat behind them had both Hilary and Alex turning to the stairs leading to the loft.

"If I may interrupt, Sir," Sergeant Hogsworth put in apologetically. "It might be best to have this conversation elsewhere." He nodded meaningfully at the glass door leading to the street.

Alex ruffled his hair in thought.

"Right," he said crisply and nudged Hilary towards the staircase. "Come on, we'll talk upstairs. Not that we've time to chat, but the fewer people aware I'm free, the better."

They trooped upstairs. Hilary could see Hogsworth thought she made an unlikely ally. She sort of had to agree.

""How long have you been here?" she inquired as she found the tea kettle singing on the stove. The left-over shrimp paella was piled on plates. Claude wound around Hogsworth's legs like an old friend.

"Long enough to figure out what you've been up to." Alan tossed the legal pad with her scribbled notes over to her. Hilary caught it automatically.

"Anybody like to fill me in on what's been happening?" she invited. "Last I heard we were all being fitted for steel bracelets."

Swiftly and concisely Alex filled her in on everything that had happened in the days since they had seen each other. Almost everything. He felt foolish admitting that he had been scaling her fire escape when he'd been nailed by Hogsworth, so he brushed over that.

He concluded, "That leaves us less than twenty-four hours to prove your friend Pauley killed Kinsale or we may still be wearing steel bracelets."

"You have no doubts Grainger is your man?"

Hogsworth, settling his bulk at the table, looked regretful. "None, Miss."

She couldn't believe it. And yet . . .

Hogsworth mumbled around a mouthful of peppers and shrimp, "You'd best tell her about that rough draft, sir."

Alex nodded. "About a month ago a painting turned up at Christies' in Hong Kong purporting to be Rembrandt's *Ruth.*"

"The painting stolen from Lord Henry's estate?"

"Right. But this painting was from an American collection. Examination revealed it to be a forgery, that's how the Yard came into it. The forgery was x-rayed and another painting discovered beneath. Or rather a rough draft of a painting which had received a bit of attention a few months earlier in a New York exhibition."

Hilary stared uncomprehendingly. "What painting?"

Alex seemed to have trouble meeting her eyes. "*Strength of the Hills.*"

"*Mine?*" Hilary set the teakettle down with a clatter on the burners. "You're telling me someone painted a copy Rembrandt over one of my old canvases?"

"That was what originally led us to believe you were part of this art scam. You and Pauley both, with Xeres acting the part of thief."

"Because someone swiped one of my canvases?"

"We thought it was probably a kind of joke on the buyers. If the painting were x-rayed they would expect to see several rough drafts, that's common with Rembrandt's stuff. But to leave your own work seemed to be thumbing your nose."

"And this would be an unconscious desire to be caught? What?"

"Supreme arrogance."

"And I strike you as the supremely arrogant type?"

"Things look different on paper. There was your close association with Pauley. The degree of skill involved in the forgeries." Alex shrugged. "Using one of your canvases does indicate access— or call it proximity—to you."

The silence crowding the loft was ominous.

"I hope you have something more solid than this to support your case against Grainger."

Alex rose and came round the counter. He would have liked to take Hilary into his arms. He did not.

He said quietly, for her ears only, "Even if I'd had an airtight case against you, it would have taken me less than five minutes to realize you couldn't possibly have been involved."

Sergeant Hogsworth cleared his throat. "This case against Pauley is quite clear, Miss, if circumstantial. Pauley sold that faked Rembrandt to the collector who sold it to Christies' in Hong Kong. We've finally got that documented."

Hilary glanced from Alan's face to Hogsworth's. She said nothing.

"Pauley owns the house in Smuggler's Bay," Alex told her. "Xeres set the meet, true enough, but why that house if Pauley wasn't involved?"

Hogsworth put in, "This was never released to the press, but the front door lock was not forced till Sir Alex broke in that night with you. Pauley told the police the realtor must have left it unlocked on his last visit."

"There's something else," Alex said, still watching Hilary's profile. "Pauley lied to you about why the sheriff first came to see him. It was strictly because a murder had been committed on his property. You and I were never mentioned at all. Why do you suppose he lied?"

To scare you off, Hilary thought numbly. *To scare me into asking you to leave.* It was dead certain Grainger had known who Alex was from the moment he had seen him. Had perhaps even expected him to turn up.

"I can't believe it," she said automatically. But she did believe it. "You're saying that Grainger tried to contract a murder."

"There's more," Alex said grimly. "It's not proof but it's a damn good start. Pauley's up to his neck in debt, that's one motive. He was about to go down as accessory to Lord Henry Archibald's murder, that's motive number two. If I'd got Xeres I'd have had Pauley as well. He knew that."

"Pauley likes power, recognition, the good life. He likes being a little tin god," Hogsworth commented. "He'd do just about anything to preserve that."

"But *murder*?" Hilary stared at them. "I've known Grainger forever. He's my rep. He's a friend. He's why I am where I am today. He's not the kind of man who goes around committing murder."

This was apparently too silly to bother answering. Alex said flatly, "You are where you are today because you are you. Because you're bloody brilliant, if you ask me. As you told me yourself not so long ago, Pauley is a businessman. He was sharp enough to spot what you were. Don't waste your loyalty on him, because he would shop you in an instant if you weren't of use to him anymore. He's a cold-blooded killer. He killed Kinsale—"

"That's not true! You don't know that!"

The both stared at her with a kind of intractable sympathy. Hilary turned away and walked agitatedly up and down the long room. She stared at the stacks of books, of canvases, she stopped before the Monet Grainger had given her for her birthday. Was even this genuine? Was anything anymore?

"You don't wish to see it so you've shut your eyes to it. Just as you've shut your eyes to Se—"

"But he'd just signed Bryan!"

"Don't be naive. If Kinsale wasn't a partner then he must have been trying his hand at blackmail. Don't you find it a bit coincidental that we start asking Kinsale questions about Xeres' connections in Steeple Hill, and the very next day Pauley, who has steadfastly refused to touch him with a stick, signs Kinsale?"

Hilary moistened her lips. The logic was inescapable.

"Just how good was Kinsale?"

"Very."

"The value of an artist's work appreciates rapidly after death, doesn't it?"

"Sometimes. Bryan isn't known though."

Alex's smile chided. "He will be when Pauley gets through. The man stands to make a tidy profit off Kinsale's work. In fact, I'd say that's motive number three. Pauley would be killing two birds with one stone."

Unfortunately it was plausible. Hilary went back and tried to pour tea with hands that were unsteady.

"Why here?" she asked finally, and with those words knew she had surrendered to the inevitable. "Why kill Bryan here?"

Absently Alex's long fingers stroked the cat now purring in his arms.

"Possibly to throw suspicion on me," he said. "Possibly it simply worked out that way. I suppose he followed Kinsale after their meeting, and I suppose the first move Kinsale would have made was to dash round here and boast his good fortune to Serena. Pauley may have followed him."

Hogsworth said, "The autopsy revealed that Kinsale had consumed a quantity of wine with lunch."

"He told us that he had a chemical intolerance for alcohol," Alex reminded her. "Even a small amount of wine would have made him very drunk, which would have made him careless and an easy target. I think Pauley got everything he wanted out of Bryan during their meeting, including a lucrative contract. He followed him over here and strangled him using wire from the storeroom."

"You think Grainger just carries contracts around with him?"

"Kinsale may have been about to attempt another spot of blackmail," Hogsworth suggested to his chief. "Given Xeres' connection to the Thomas girl and Kinsale's feelings for her."

It was clear the two of them had the whole thing calculated to the last detail, Hilary reflected catching the warning look Alex shot his sergeant. But this was where their nothing-but-the-facts-ma'am approach got them into trouble. Serena knew Grainger and had once had a relationship with Xeres, *ipso facto* Serena was criminally involved. What did these two imagine she was doing? Making de-coder rings for the gang?

And then the truth of it hit Hilary between the eyes. Not Serena. *Selena.* Selena, who by virtue of Serena's relationship, also knew Xeres. Selena the business woman, the graphic artist who had painted a startling facsimile of the Notre Dame Cathedral on her living room wall. Selena who was undistracted by romantic affairs, who had an 'alibi' for Bryan's death and who, having 'shopped' Hilary and Alex to the police, had weakened and come to warn them at the last moment. *Selena*, thought Hilary. *My closest friend. Please not Selena.*

She pressed her lips together afraid the words would somehow escape.

Grainger was bad enough. Despite their long friendship, Hilary knew in her bones Alex was right about Grainger. He had always done his best for her, but Hilary had recognized years ago that Grainger was selfish, egotistical and potentially ruthless. The only thing Hilary could imagine Grainger loving more than himself was Art.

"How are you going to prove any of this?"

Hogsworth and Alex exchanged a look. A Boys Only Clubhouse kind of thing.

"We need evidence," Alex said.

"No kidding."

"Something that will hold up in court."

Hilary contemplated them without emotion. After a moment she looked down and finished pouring the tea, her hands now steady. "Why don't I call Grainger and tell him I know he killed Bryan? When he comes after me you two can nab him in the act."

Alex stared at her. Gaped might be a better word. It was certainly not an expression she had seen on his lean ascetic face before. "Are you out of your mind?" he inquired politely after a moment.

Hogsworth said regretfully, "Unless he actually killed you, Miss, it wouldn't prove much. Not about Kinsale's murder or Pauley's involvement in lord Henry's death. And attempted murder is a difficult charge to make stick."

"But maybe I could get a taped confession like they do in the movies?"

Hogsworth seemed to weigh the pros and cons of this while Alex fumed, "Are you *daft?* This is sheer—sheer drivel. We've already worked out what we're doing. We're going to break into the gallery tonight and find the proof we need."

"Oh. But I'm out of *my* mind?" Hilary shook her head. "Has it occurred to you—even considering that the proof would actually be where you could find it—that Grainger has a slightly more sophisticated security set up than you've run into lately?"

"I sussed out the security system when we were in the gallery for your birthday party. The outside doors rely on electronic locks activated by ID cards with key-override in case of power failure. The inside doors are secured by an electronic key pad. Isn't that right?"

"Correct," Hilary said. "Now tell me how you plan to get past all that hardware?"

"The first night I spent here you mentioned you taught a class at the gallery. That means you have access to at least the perimeter doors."

Hilary blinked. Her art classes seemed a lifetime ago.

"That's true. I do. In fact I was supposed to teach this evening. I canceled."

"Uncancel."

"Just like that?"

Alex smiled.

"And what happens once we're inside the gallery?"

He shrugged. "We'll burn that bridge when we come to it."

Hilary was afraid that was true.

***

The plan was running like clockwork, Hilary thought to herself, putting the final sweeps of charcoal to the reclining nude on her sketchpad.

She gazed past the circle of bent heads to the corridor beyond. All was quiet. Not so much as a gliding shadow or muffled foot fall to reveal that Alex and Hogsworth were prowling through the show and work rooms of the gallery searching for proof connecting Grainger with stolen or forged paintings—and—

Bryan's murder.

Hilary's eight students scratched away in silent concentration. Hilary circled them, unobtrusively peeking at her watch. Still another ten minutes before she could reasonably call an end to the session. With half-attention she answered questions, gave criticism where requested.

She was afraid this was all a waste of time. Grainger would never be so careless as to leave incriminating materials on the premises. Yet where better to hide a workshop, Alex had pointed out, than in another workshop? If there is anything here, Hilary told herself, it's behind locked doors—not that locked doors would stop Alex in the mood he was in.

The minutes ticked by so quietly she could hear them on her watch.

"That's it everyone. Let's call it a night."

Slowly the students packed away their paraphernalia, talking, joking. Hilary could hardly restrain herself from pushing them out the door. Out of the corner of her eye she watched the model stretch and wander off to dress. Hilary hoped she didn't bump into Hogsworth or Alex.

Tonight the students' chatter was mostly of Bryan's murder. They spoke casually of the disruptive presence of the police, complained of reporters from the bigger newspapers who had over-run Steeple Hill. Hilary tried to concentrate, her nerves strung to screaming pitch by the time she saw the last student out and locked the glass doors behind him.

Switching out the mains, she went looking for her co-conspirators in the eerie green gloom of the exit lights.

At night the gallery seemed to take on a wax museum sort of creepiness. Hilary's footsteps sounded soft and secretive even to herself as she started up the wide staircase. The dozen eyes of an abstract painting followed her slow ascent.

The very silence seemed a live, listening thing.

Hilary reached the second floor, her steps falling away in the thick carpet.

"Alex?" she called quietly. "Sergeant Hogsworth?"

There was no answer.

Hilary paused in the doorway of the upper gallery with its polished floors gleaming from the moon in the skylight. She spied the dim outline of paintings all down the wall. At the far end of the long room she could see light shining from a small anteroom.

Hilary's rubber-soled shoes made no sound on the tile floors.

"We're not completely wasting our time," she heard Alex speaking in normal tones from the anteroom.

Hogsworth grunted assent.

"They must have kept the workshop in the warehouse cellar, but they stored the paintings here. I'd wager a week's pay this paint scraping is going to prove *La Bohemienne* red."

"Ah," rumbled Hogsworth. "From the Louvres stolen Hals?"

"Exactly."

Alex glanced up as Hilary appeared in the doorway.

"Any luck?" she inquired.

"Some."

He finished neatly labeling a small brown paper sack containing, as far as Hilary could tell, nothing more than a fleck of red paint.

Hogsworth was half-under the sink in the far corner studying the baseboard with a magnifying glass.

"Are you about finished here?"

"Nearly done." Alex assured her. "Sam can finish up. Why don't you and I go downstairs and scope out Pauley's office?"

She knew it was silly, but Hilary wished he would whisper. She couldn't help feeling someone was watching and listening to them.

"I'm not sure that's such a good idea now. What if we trigger the alarm? Or what if Grainger comes back for some reason? We probably can't get in anyway. I don't know the code . . ."

"Panicking?" Alex guided Hilary out through the darkened passage.

The weight of his hand on the small of her back steadied her. "Is Sir Alex married?" she had casually asked Hogsworth while they waited in the car that afternoon.

Hogsworth had seemed to find the question comical.

"Sir Alex? Lord love you, Miss! He's a born bachelor, as Mrs. H. Always says. Not that there aren't plenty of lovelies who've tried, but he's a canny one, Sir Alex. Married to the Yard, I suppose."

The sergeant was a fount of information regarding Alex.

It was Hogsworth who told Hilary about the trap Alex had laid with his godfather and former mentor, Lord Henry. Alex had been after Xeres for some time in connection with a rash of art thefts, but it had been lord Henry's idea to use his own Rembrandt as bait. Unfortunately something had gone disastrously wrong. Breaking his pattern, the thief had struck early in the evening, Lord Henry had been killed and Alex held himself to blame.

At this point in his narrative Hogsworth had pulled out a hand-kerchief the size of the British flag and blown his nose mightily. Hilary gathered that in his own phlegmatic way the sergeant was deeply moved. Whether at Lord Henry's demise or its effect on Sir Alex was not clear. Alex, she pieced together, had not been able to let the law take its course. Eaten alive with guilt he had hounded and harassed Xeres, knowing him culpable but unable to prove it. He had been perilously close to an official reprimand when he abruptly chose to make use of several weeks of back holidays. The next thing Hogsworth heard, his chief had been found slain in a house on the California coast.

This cleared up several points for Hilary although it didn't strike her as a healthy sign that Hogsworth was the one filling her in on Alex's history, certain though she was that Hogsworth would never confide anything he believed his Super would not want known.

The problem was (and as their problems went it was a minor one, granted) Alex was not talking to her. He was not explaining anything. Three days and nights might be long enough to fall in love but it wasn't long enough to build any kind of understanding. Hilary was confident enough not to need a lot of reassurance; she believed they did have an understanding, but Alex had yet to indicate he felt the same way now that he had his memory back.

Anyway, Hilary sternly reminded herself, I'm a big girl now. A modern woman. I told him he didn't have to make guarantees or promises.

"Piece of cake," Alex informed her.

"Huh?" Hilary came back to reality to find they were standing before Grainger's locked office door.

"I'm familiar with this model." Alex activated the keypad on the wall. Hilary stared at the blocks of glowing red numerals, which appeared.

"A six digit code," Alex muttered. "We should have three tries before the alarm goes off. What's Pauley's birthday?"

"July sixteenth, nineteen forty-five," Hilary responded after a moment's calculation. "Why?"

"Generally with a six digit code people go for a significant date. Birthdays are most common."

Alex punched the numbers into the keypad. A light at the top flashed red and a warning beep rang out, loud in the gallery's hush.

"Damn." Alex turned back to Hilary. "What's another important date to Pauley. Some kind of anniversary. When did the gallery open?"

"This one or the one in New York? The New York gallery came first."

"You tell me."

"New York is the larger of the two, the more prestigious, but this is Grainger's home base."

"Has he ever referred to either date?"

"No, but I remember the date the New York branch opened

from one of those articles in Napier's—" Hilary shook her head. "I should say *your* hotel room. I keep thinking of Napier as someone else."

"What's the date?"

"January eleventh nineteen seventy-one."

Alex typed in the numbers. There was a tense pause and then the red light flared and that ominous beep sounded once more.

"That's it," said Hilary. "We don't dare risk tripping the alarm."

"We have less than sixteen hours left," Alex reminded her. "We've got to risk it."

"He's not going to leave anything incriminating here," Hilary argued. "What do you imagine we'll find?"

"I'm not sure. He must keep some kind of records. Possibly another set of books."

"But he won't have left those for the police to find. If such records exist, they'll be inside a safe."

"One problem at a time."

Alex's certainty was unnerving. Without his memory 'Alan' had been a little less confident. A little more cautious. Easier to love. Alex was almost exhaustingly sure of himself. A man who needed nothing from anyone—except the right code numbers.

"Do you know the date this gallery opened?"

"I'm not sure."

"Think."

"I am thinking!" Hilary could feel her forehead breaking out in sweat. "I think it coincided with his birthday, but I can't remember the year. Try July sixteenth, nineteen—nineteen—oh, God, what year *was* it? Seventy-eight? Seventy-seven?" She shut her eyes trying to remember.

She could feel Alex's restiveness.

"Seventy-eight. I'm almost positive."

Alex called up the numbers once more.

"*Wait!*"

Hilary's gasp stopped Alex's finger a fraction from the key pad. "Try this: 061063."

Alex's eyes assessed. Then he obeyed.

The second after he pushed the last digit the light at the top flashed green. The door to Grainger's office unlocked with a loud click in the gallery's emptiness.

Alex reached for the handle and pushed open the door.

"Mind telling me exactly what that date was?" he inquired.

Hilary grinned wryly. "The day Grainger had his photo taken with Picasso."

CHAPTER FOURTEEN

"Nothing," Hilary said in disgust, closing the last of the ledgers stacked in front of her. "Any paper trail that may have existed is long gone. If it ever existed."

"It existed all right." Alex slapped a file down on Grainger's desktop. "Damn. Damn. Damn. We're too late, that's what it boils down to. He's already begun the mop up."

Hilary pushed a hand through her hair. She glanced across at Alex and saw him rake impatient fingers though his own dark waves. He caught her eyes, read her look and grinned.

"Snap."

Despite his weariness and frustration, Alex's smile lightened Hilary's heart. Whatever happens she thought, I'd do it all again.

"One good thing," she pointed out, "You've put an end to their operation. Xeres is dead and Grainger's closed up shop. He's covering his tracks as fast as he can."

Alex slid off horn-rimmed reading glasses and rubbed his eyes. The glasses made him look older, more conservative. It had startled Hilary to look across and see a stranger sitting there.

But that reluctant grin was all Alan's. So was the intent green stare he directed her way now and again. It made Hilary feel ridiculously happy—and self-conscious with Sergeant Hogsworth hovering in the wings like a suspicious chaperon.

"It's not good enough," Alex was muttering. "Two men dead. Three, if you want to count Xeres. Even if these cowboys can't pin a murder charge on me this will ruin my career. And you're in a tight spot as well, luv. Pauley knows you suspect him. I think sooner or later he might try to . . . make sure of you."

"What does that mean? You think Grainger might try to . . . arrange an accident?"

Alex's eyes held her own. "A murderer's conscience is an uneasy animal. It feels threatened all the time."

Hilary had no answer to that. Alex said such brutal things casually. As though it were natural that people should turn to murder to solve their problems. They held such different ideas of the world.

Sergeant Hogsworth ducked his head in the office door.

"It may be nothing, sir, but a car's pulled up outside."

A startled squeak escaped Hilary. Both Hogsworth and Alex looked her way.

"You were saying?" Alex asked politely.

"I was saying let's get the heck out of here!"

"Not a bad notion, sir."

"Twelve hours left," Alex said, glancing at the clock on Grainger's desk. He began dumping files back in the open file cabinet drawer. "Any brilliant ideas? Whatever records Pauley kept of his back door transactions are ashes now. There's no murder weapon to speak of. We've got to have physical evidence, but what?"

Shoving the ledgers back on to the shelves Hilary threw over her shoulder, "What's the point? What's left? If we can't find any proof that Grainger was involved in the sale of stolen paintings, how can we prove he was involved in murder?"

Alex slammed shut the file drawer. Lifting the ledgers from Hilary's arms he shoved them on the shelf in one block.

"They've got to be in order," Hilary protested. "Otherwise Grainger will know."

"Better get a move on, sir," Hogsworth suggested, reappearing in the office door.

Over the thudding of her heart Hilary caught the look Alex and his sergeant exchanged before Alex snapped out the green desk lamp. *I think they're enjoying this!*

"Come on," Alex whispered, taking Hilary's hand. His touch comforted her in the darkness. His fingers wrapped warmly about hers as he guided her around the desk and out of the office.

Alex pulled the door close behind them. Hilary saw the red sentinel eye spring into watchfulness behind them.

Hands still linked they ran soundlessly across the gleaming marble floors though shadows cast by the towering sculptures and support columns.

***

By the time they reached the outside exit Hogsworth was in the rental car, warming its engine.

Hilary scrambled into the back seat. Alex pulled shut the door, and they were off.

"Pull around front," Alex ordered. "I want to see who our midnight caller is."

Slowly they rounded the corner. The yellow Mercedes convertible parked before the gallery steps was empty.

"Grainger," Hilary said without surprise.

"Interesting. I wonder what he's afraid he might have left behind."

"Why don't we ask him?"

Alex's grin was a gleam in the darkness. "What do you suggest we do, beat it out of him?"

"Of course not. But we could watch him. Follow him. If Grainger's afraid . . ."

"Grainger will be afraid from now on. That's what makes Grainger so dangerous. Fear is what made him kill Kinsale."

Hogsworth chimed in, "That's the thing about murderers, Miss. They can never leave well enough alone. They keep remembering things, you see."

Hilary stared. "You mean there's nothing there?"

"Nothing that we could find and we've been searching for close on nine hours."

Grainger's car disappeared behind them as they turned down the tree-lined street.

"What are we going to do then?" Hilary demanded. "There

must be some proof we can find. We can't just give up and wait to be arrested."

Neither man answered. By some silent communication Hogsworth turned into Fan Shell Park and stopped the car in the deserted lot. With the engine off it was very quiet. The car smelt of pipe tobacco and a faint woodsy aftershave that Hilary remembered from Alex's hotel room at the Seven Palms.

The minutes ticked by. Hogsworth absently twisted the ends of his handlebar mustache. Alex's finger drummed restlessly on the dashboard.

Hilary was surprised when he reached back and found her hand, his thumb tracing the ridge of her knuckles. There was something soothing in that absent-minded caress.

Hilary sat bolt upright. "What about their inventory?"

Alex's thumb paused. Hogsworth stopped twisting his mustache ends. They both turned to her.

"Where are all these stolen paintings? Where are the forged copies?"

"What do you mean?"

"After Lord Henry's murder and the discovery of that faked Rembrandt in Hong Kong things must have got pretty hot. They would have had to wait to move the rest of the paintings, wouldn't they?"

"The originals could still be sold," Alex replied. "Pauley would have to move fast and he'd have to be very discreet, but I'm betting he unloaded them weeks ago. Even if at a dead loss. He couldn't risk having them found."

"They would never keep much of an inventory anyway," Hogsworth informed her. "Too dicey. There was always about three months between jobs."

"Time enough to knock off two or three copies at a few million pounds each."

"But it hasn't been three months since Lord Henry's *Ruth* was stolen," Hilary pointed out. "It's been one month. And less than a month ago the first forgery showed up in Hong Kong. So where are the other copies?"

"Maybe they don't exist." Alex sounded weary. "Maybe they were never painted."

"They were painted. They couldn't sell the original till the forgeries were completed. Otherwise what was it all for?"

"Then they were destroyed," Alex asserted. "Keeping the forgeries would be tantamount to a signed confession. They are burned or at the bottom of the sea."

"No way." Hilary squeezed Alex's shoulder. "Two or three million dollars? Grainger would never in a hundred years burn that kind of money. This whole scam was a gamble from the start. Do you honestly believe Grainger wouldn't gamble that he couldn't successfully hide those paintings?"

"She's got a point, sir," Hogsworth said. "Pauley's the bloke to think he could outsmart us all."

"I don't mean to burst your bubble," Alex said acridly, "but I had thought of this myself. The fact is I've already looked for the paintings. I searched the house at Smuggler's Bay yesterday."

"What abut the cliffs? Smugglers used to—"

"I spent hours searching the caves in the cliffs. There was nothing there. Today Hogsworth and I both searched the warehouse while you were playing twenty questions with Selena, and tonight we all searched the gallery." Alex paused for breath. "Even Pauley's not mad enough to hide the forgeries in his own home. I'm telling you, to keep himself out of prison the man would have burned the original Rembrandt, let alone the fakes. They no longer exist."

Hilary said nothing.

Into the silence came the slow, melodious chimes of the Steeple Hill bell tolling the hour.

Hilary smiled. "Yes, they do," she said very calmly. "And I know where they are."

***

Etched in black relief against the giant moon stood Steeple Hill's chapel. Night was kind to its peeling paint and missing boards. Moonlight bathed the snaggle-tooth fence and broken tombstones in silver radiance, lending a touch of unearthliness.

It was not until they were a few yards away, crunching their way up the broken walk, that the boarded windows became obvious. Weeds and wildflowers choked the path, rustling spookily in the stillness.

"Doesn't look as though it's been used in years," Sergeant Hogsworth said, bringing up the rear.

"It hasn't," Hilary returned. "That's why it's perfect. No one comes here anymore. It's even too far off the path for teen vandals." Her foot slipped on an over-turned stone and Alex steadied her, hand on her arm.

He managed to make her feel fragile and protected at the same time. She was neither, so it was a pleasant novelty.

"What about the bell?" Alex asked.

They all stared up at the black window of the steeple gaping like a mouth with its tongue torn out.

"Sold years ago. The chimes are recorded and broadcast from downtown."

As they reached the sagging front porch, Hilary began to have doubts. The chapel looked as though it hadn't been disturbed in a century. Alex pulled experimentally at the planks barricading the entrance. Nothing budged. If anyone had entered the chapel it had not been through here.

Hilary went around the side of the building, scrutinizing the row of boarded-up windows.

"Of course I could be wrong . . ." she muttered, observing a mouse scurry across the stoop and disappear through a crack in the door with a flick of its tail.

Alex bent closer and gave a low whistle. "Take a look, Sam."

Hogsworth moved past Hilary to inspect the boards Alex pointed out.

"Well well," he rumbled.

Alex drew Hilary closer. "Look."

Hilary's gaze followed Alex's finger. Instantly she saw what he meant. The nail heads gleaming in the weathered boards shone bright silver.

"They've been here a day at most," Alex said thinking aloud.

His eyes met Hilary's and he grinned an uncharacteristically boyish grin. All the weariness and strain seemed magically lifted from his features. At last they were on the right track; relief made him look years younger.

"By George, I think she's got it," he informed his sergeant in a creditable imitation of Rex Harrison.

"By George, I think you're right, sir."

The three of them laughed in silly relief.

Hogsworth returned to the car to get the makeshift tools they had fetched from the warehouse. Hilary turned to find Alex studying her

"Alone at last," he drawled.

She chuckled.

Alex rubbed the side of his nose with his index finger.

"Have I been assuming too much?"

"What do you mean?" Hilary returned. "What is it you're assuming?"

"Us."

His eyes were unreadable in the moonlight.

Hilary swallowed against the sudden fluttering sensation in her throat.

"I'm useless at this kind of thing," Alex continued almost impatiently. "I suppose you want it all dotted and crossed. Women usually do."

"Had a lot of experience have you?"

"Enough."

"So your sergeant mentioned," she retorted.

"I just hadn't met the right lady," Alex said simply without a hint of that practiced charm.

It dawned on Hilary that Alex, for all his vaunted experience, wasn't any more comfortable with unvarnished emotion than she. There are all different kinds of firsts. If Hogsworth knew his stuff, then Alex had not made room in his life for real relationships any more than Hilary had.

The moment to respond was lost however, as Hogsworth came marching back whistling "A Hymn to Him" from *My Fair Lady*.

Alex and his DS made short work of the planks blocking the entrance. The door behind the boards was worm-eaten though and gave easily, hinges groaning in true haunted house fashion. The chapel interior was black as midnight. A cloud of dust mingled with the odor of mildew and generations of rodents rose to meet them.

Hilary shivered inside her jacket, following the two men; their flashlight beams played across the chunks of fallen plaster and years of dirt and weeds covering the rotting floor. She stared curiously.

The pews had been torn out and sold ages ago with the altar, railings and other furnishings, but the carved posts and lintels stood as testament to a former Spartan beauty.

A trail of footprints vanished in the thick dust just outside the ring of their flashlight beams.

"Doesn't look like there's any place to hide," Hogsworth said. His whisper boomed down the empty room.

"We're looking for some kind of container, probably metal," Hilary answered. "It might be cylindrical, but maybe not. The only certainty is that it will be waterproof and airtight to protect the paintings."

Alex climbed over the rubble to the foot of the steeple stairs. "Sam, you take the vestry," he ordered. "Hilary, take this room. There are any number of niches he could have stashed a box."

"Wait, I'll take the steeple," Hilary said quickly, moving to head Alex off. "Those stairs will never hold your weight, Alex."

"They took Pauley's weight; they'll take mine." The first step cracked warningly beneath his foot.

"Don't be crazy," Hilary told him. She dodged under Alex's arm and ran lightly up the first two stairs.

"Hilary, get back here!" Alex commanded.

He started forward again but was halted by the foreboding sound of splitting wood.

"Just give me a minute . . ." Cautiously Hilary continued her climb. Reaching the top of the stairs, she swung the flashlight in an arc around the narrow room. The ray of light revealed nothing more sinister than termites at work.

"Nothing down here, sir," Hogsworth reported, returning to where Alex waited fuming at the foot of the rotting staircase. "Blimey." He followed Alex's gaze. "She's never gone up there?" Hogsworth brushed absently at a cobweb draped over his shoulder.

"She has," Alex said through his teeth.

"She's a game little thing," Hogsworth said with unwilling admiration. "Then with a glance at his Super's face, "Good God, sir, don't tell me *you've—*"

"Shut up, Sam," Alex bit out. He raised his head and yelled, "Hilary, what the *hell* are you doing up there?"

"Having tea, old boy," Hilary's voice floated down. "What do you think I'm doing?"

Fortunately Alex's under-breath reply was lost to the history books.

Once more Hilary guided the flashlight beam around the small room. There was nothing here. Nothing but the remains of bird nests and animal droppings.

She would have bet anything. . . .

Hilary swung the flashlight above her head. She couldn't help the gasp of horror that escaped as the ray caught rows and rows of beady, unwinking eyes. The rafters appeared to be coated in furry bodies. Dozens of bats hung from the tower ceiling. As the glare from the flashlight hit them, the brown mass began to ripple and undulate.

The next instant a cloud of squeaking flapping vermin had taken wing.

Hilary screamed and ducked, covering her head as dust and bats flew about her.

"*Hilary!*" cried Alex from down below.

Once more he tried the stairs.

A few feet up there came a horrendous tearing sound, and the entire wooden staircase separated from the wall.

Alex reached out to brace himself as the staircase buckled. He half-fell between the wall and the stairs. With desperate strength he clawed his way onto the shivering staircase. Hogsworth caught his legs and dragged him back to safety. Chunks of plaster and wood and debris crashed down around them.

"There's a rope in the car." Alex clambered awkwardly to his feet and pulled his dust-caked sergeant up. "Hurry."

Hogsworth disappeared without a word.

"Hilary!"

No answer as the shudders and shrieks of the old building subsided into groaning stillness.

"Hilary, for God's sake answer me!" Alex's voice cracked on the last word. Where the hell was Hogsworth? Why had he let her go up? If anything happened to her . . .

"I'm okay." Her voice sounded odd, disembodied. "There are bats in the belfry."

To his unutterable relief Hilary appeared in the spotlight of his torch where the stairs had once connected to the tower. Her dark hair stood on end and was gray with dust. Her eyes glimmered with diamond brilliance. She held a long, conical container in one hand and what appeared to be rolled oilskin in the other.

"It was jammed up where the bell used to be fastened," she said in a funny shaky voice. "Just one painting. He couldn't bring himself to destroy it." She reached up and dashed the tears spilling over her cheeks. "It's the original, Alex. It's *Ruth*."

***

"Spectacular, isn't it?" Grainger commented conversationally from behind them.

Alex wheeled only to be stopped cold by the sight of the snub-nose automatic aimed at his chest.

"Nothing," Grainger informed him, "would give me greater

pleasure than to blow your goddamn head off." His eyes rose briefly to Hilary's motionless figure.

"Hilary, my pet, put the painting back in the cylinder and toss it down."

"Don't do it, Hilary," Alex warned.

Grainger's finger appeared to fractionally tighten on the trigger and Hilary hastily crammed the rolled painting back into the canister.

"Gently my pet," exclaimed Grainger. "Think of what you hold in your hands."

Alex's life.

"Where's my sergeant?" Alex sounded calm and cold. He showed none of the panic Hilary felt, but then he didn't really know Grainger.

Grainger's eyes swerved back to Alex. "Your sergeant is catching up on his much needed beauty rest. You'll find him beside your car. If I decide to let you live."

Hilary finished recapping the container with unsteady fingers. "Here, Grainger."

"You killed Kinsale, didn't you?" Alex interjected quickly, stalling for time.

Grainger's smile grew ironic. "I'm afraid that only works in movies. Throw the canister down, Hilary. I've got a plane to catch."

"You amaze me, Pauley," Alex sneered. "I though you'd want to impress Hilary with your brilliance. The over-weaning conceit of the murderer and all that."

"You know," Grainger reflected, still unruffled. "I don't think you realize how close I am to putting a bullet in your brain. Especially as I have nothing to lose at this point."

"Because you lost your head and killed Kinsale."

Grainger shrugged. "It was a gamble. He didn't leave me much choice, I'm afraid. He had the unmitigated gall to think he could blackmail me. He also planned to blackmail Serena into becoming his mistress."

"Serena?" Hilary echoed hollowly.

Grainger tittered. "I'm afraid as usual he had his facts con-fused. Wrong sister." He shrugged. "Anyway they can only hang me once—and they really don't go in for that these days, do they? Besides, they'd have to catch me and they won't. By this time tomorrow I'll be on my ranch in South America."

He smiled at Alex who continued to watch him with narrowed eyes, waiting for his chance.

"So you see, *old boy*, the only thing stopping me from sending you straight to hell is my foolish affection for Hilary. And frankly I think she would be better off—"

Hilary tossed the canister down and Granger moved to get it, his eyes never wavering from Alex's taut figure.

"Thank you, my pet." He gave Alex another of those frosty smiles.

"Not that I wouldn't love to stay and gratify your curiosity, but you've probably figured most of it out. Everything fell apart after that fool Xeres killed your old crony Archibald. You really were quite persistent. Alan panicked. So when you chased him over here we came up with a very simple plan."

"Xeres was to take me out at Smuggler's Bay."

"You didn't really think he was going to cut a deal?" Grainger shook his head. "I drove Xeres to the house as planned and then waited on the ridge for his signal. We planned to stuff your body in your car and drive the car off the cliff road. Then I'd have taken Alan straight to the airport."

Grainger sighed with real regret. "So simple. We just didn't count on one thing. Well, two actually."

"I didn't rent a car," said Alex.

"And why on earth not?" Grainger still sounded exasperated. "Why come by taxi? Now who would have thought of that? And then of course you killed Xeres, which really screwed things up."

Hilary recognized that Grainger was off and running. Even now he couldn't resist the sound of his own voice.

"I waited and waited," he continued peevishly. "Finally I saw the taxi driver go into the house and then come running out to radio for help. I drove off. Of course I knew about the back stairs to the beach. I kept an eye out, and sure enough I spotted you stumbling along. Unfortunately there were too many people around."

"You must have seen him get on the bus for Steeple Hill," Hilary said. "You must have been waiting for him when we arrived."

"I followed you into the park but there were still too many people. Then to make matters worse Hilary showed up."

Grainger glanced up fleetingly to where Hilary stood.

"It was obvious something wasn't kosher. You'd left the scene of a crime, you were acting strangely, as though you were drunk or injured. But what could I do? I had to arrange my own alibi. I went back to the gallery where I was still 'working late' by the time Hilary arrived for her evening class.

Hilary recalled something. "It was you at the warehouse that night, wasn't it? Arguing with Selena in the workroom."

Grainger nodded. "The police came to see me about the body in my house at Smuggler's Bay. It wasn't hard to put two and two together. I told Selena that Hilary's 'Alan' was a Scotland Yard cop hot on our trail and that Xeres had fled the country after killing your—" he nodded to Alex "partner."

"Quick thinking."

"I thought so. I warned Selena to be very careful; that you were using Hilary to get to us. The next day I followed you to market Street. If I'd had one clean shot at a hit and run I'd have taken it but it never happened. I had to give up."

Grainger's irritation with the inconvenience of thwarted homicide plans made Hilary's blood run cold.

"When I actually came face to face with you at Hilary's party I realized you hadn't a clue who I was. The so-clever, so-persistent Sir Alexander Napier had amnesia!" Grainger laughed disbelievingly. "It was the first break I'd had in months. Naturally I tried my damnedest to throw suspicion on *you*. Sadly it didn't quite pan out." Grainger shrugged and peered at his watch. "Anyway, *que sera* as we say in South America."

He began to back towards the front entrance of the chapel, the automatic never wavering from its position on Alex.

With all her heart Hilary prayed that Alex wouldn't move. She could feel tension radiating from him. She knew he was weighing the odds, trying to decide how quick Grainger's reflexes were, how good a shot he was. Hilary knew Grainger's reflexes, baring the moral ones, were excellent, and she knew nothing on earth would stop him killing Alex if Alex so much as twitched.

Her attention was caught by movement in the doorway behind Grainger.

Hogsworth?

No, there was more than one figure slipping soundlessly into the chapel behind Grainger.

"Adieu, my pet," Grainger called and tucked the metal cylinder beneath his arm. He reached with his free hand to feel for the doorframe, his pale eyes never leaving Alex's still figure. He seemed to hesitate. A faint smile curved his mouth as he steadied the gun.

From behind Grainger Hilary saw a flash of silver. There was a metallic click as a handcuff was snapped over Grainger's free wrist.

"Wha—?" Startled Grainger half-turned and nearly over-balanced. The next minute four deputies had wrestled him to the floor and disarmed him.

Sheriff Huntsinger sauntered forward tossing over his shoulder, "Read him his rights, Chavez."

The blonde assistant sheriff picked herself up off the filthy floor.

Almost jauntily Huntsinger saluted two fingers to Hilary still stationed at the head of the missing staircase.

To Alex he said, "That's the way we do it here in the good old U.S. of A."

"You took your sweet time," Alex shot back. "How long do you suppose I could keep him talking?"

"Don't pretend you knew we were out there," howled Huntsinger. "You couldn't have known we were following you!"

"You're right," admitted Alex, his tired smile finding Hilary. "I couldn't be sure. Next time I'll have more faith."

***

Hilary was asleep, her face buried in Alex's shoulder when they reached the warehouse the next morning. Alex was glad she was sleeping because as they pulled up to the curb two deputy sheriffs were escorting Selena out in handcuffs.

Alex bent his head and dropped a butterfly of a kiss on Hilary's ruffled hair. She had had a hell of a night. They both had. Alex hadn't been able to relax until the local fire department had deposited Hilary, filthy but unharmed, back in his arms. For the first time in his life he hadn't given a damn what happened to a national treasure.

As light as his kiss was Hilary stirred beneath it. Her eyes fluttered open. Her lips parted. Alex's eyes followed her reluctant return to consciousness. This was his first time watching Hilary wake. He hoped it wouldn't be the last.

"Are we home?" she mumbled.

His mouth curved. Out of the corner of his eye he saw the small group in front of the warehouse heading towards the black and white cars. He leaned forward, his mouth covering Hilary's, his head blocking her view of the sidewalk.

Hilary responded sweetly. Alex's heart turned over in his chest.

In the front seat Hogsworth, head bandaged, glanced in the rearview and cleared his throat uneasily.

That sound jerked Hilary back into awareness. She sat up in Alex's arms in time to see Selena being led past the car by two sheriffs.

The small sound that escaped her was something Alex would have given a bit to prevent. He knew she simply had not had time to think this part through. He dreaded, but was unsurprised, as she stiffened in his arms and turned that wide accusing stare on him.

Partly to avoid her gaze Alex looked away, meeting Selena's hard, tawny gaze.

Her red slash of a mouth was a straight angry line, the kohl-rimmed eyes glimmered with angry tears. Oh hell, thought Alex.

Hilary caught her breath.

Kohl rimmed? thought Alex.

The younger bird Serena was the one who went in for the Egyptian eyes. Selena favored the red gooey lips. So which sister . . .?

Alex half-turned, eyes following that rigid back marching away between two khaki-uniformed officers.

Hilary's hand closed over his. "Don't. Please."

"They've got the wrong girl."

"Not for long. They'll realize soon enough. Let them do it."

"Let who do it? Let them *get away* with—" Alex brushed this aside and reached for the door handle. Hilary's hands clung to his. He refused to wrestle with her under Hogsworth's astonished gaze.

"Serena's giving her a chance, that's all," Hilary pleaded, her words falling over themselves in her desperate haste. "Selena never killed anyone, Alex. You know that she never even knew about Lord Henry. She would never have gone along with murder. All she did was copy paintings. It was wrong, it was stupid, it was criminal, but she's lost everything now. Isn't that punishment enough?"

"Hilary, I'm an officer of the law. I can't simply—you can't ask me to—"

"I *am* asking you. I know I have no right, but Alex if I mean anything to you at all . . . she's my closet friend in the world. If I hadn't helped you this would never have happened. Please, Alex, when she thought the police were after you she gave us a chance."

"Sir?" Sergeant Hogsworth had his door open , one foot already on the pavement.

Alex's eyes held Hilary's.

Surely if anyone understood the difference between good and evil, between right and wrong . . .?

But she doesn't understand, he thought. He didn't *enjoy* this.

He didn't make the law. If he had a choice . . . Alex stared into the fierce blue of Hilary's tear-glazed eyes and thought despairingly that even if she did understand she would never forgive her own part in Selena's destruction. Her guilt and grief would poison everything between them. And suddenly Alex knew that he would be right as always, and he would win another laurel in his already brilliant career, but he would lose Hilary.

What had he imagined? That they would fly off into the sunset together? They were from different worlds. It would never work.

He believed in the law, in man's justice. She believed in a higher power, in the slow grind of the mills of God, or some such thing.

He would lose her. Lose her laughter, her passion. She was not the kind of woman he had ever envisioned as his wife, but she was strong, loyal, brave. She was beautiful. She would be beautiful when there was silver in her hair and lines around her sea-blue eyes. She did not look at the world as he did. He did not understand her kind of faith. He would lose that too—her faith. In life. In him. He would lose her friendship. Her love.

"Let her go," Alex said quietly.

"Sir?"

"I said, leave it," he said harshly for fear he might change his mind again.

A few hours, he told himself, would not make a difference, whatever Hilary believed. But they would make all the difference to his future with Hilary. Selena was not trained for life on the run. She would never make it. But he would give her her chance as Hilary had given him his.

"Thank you," Hilary breathed. She closed her eyes for a moment as though offering a quick prayer.

Prayers for a crook? He couldn't understand her. But *God* how he wanted her to.

Absently Alex stroked her back. He pressed his bristling cheek against her soft one.

"I won't ask you for anything else."

"Ask what you like my darling. I may not always say yes, but I want you to ask."

Alex's eyes found Hogsworth's in the mirror. He signaled his sergeant to get out of the car.

Silent moments passed after the door closed behind the sergeant. Alex closed his eyes. He thought of his carefully planned life, his passion for law and order. He thought of all the sensible choices he had made right up until he walked through the door of the house at Smuggler's Bay.

He said slowly, "Do you suppose Claude will survive quarantine?"

He opened his eyes as Hilary raised her head. Alex's smile was wry. It held a hint of something that in another man would have been uncertainty. Hilary studied him from beneath her wet lashes.

"Do you at least believe in fate?" she asked finally.

"I suppose so. What do you mean?"

"I don't think it was coincidence that the painting we found last night was of Ruth."

Alex's dark brows drew together. He studied Hilary for a moment, then a faint smile tugged at his mouth.

"No?"

Hilary reached up and pulled Alex's head down to hers.

She felt his smile widen beneath her lips as she kissed him murmuring, "Wither thou goest?"